DYING TO LIVE... AGAIN

L. F. EARL AND S. L. EARL

ISBN: 1542710227
ISBN 13: 9781542710220
Library of Congress Control Number: 2017900988
CreateSpace Independent Publishing Platform
North Charleston, South Carolina

TABLE OF CONTENTS

ACKNOWLEDGMENTS

Thanks to our family for the enduring support and love through this process.
You made this possible.

PROLOGUE

"Good grief! How much longer is Father Odom going to continue talking? Didn't he already do a sermon inside the chapel? Ugh! It's freaking twenty-seven degrees, it's wet, and the wind is blowing through my clothes." Pete's breath frosted in the cold air with every word. Realizing his words hadn't incited a response from his coworker, he continued talking. "I'm cold and hungry, and I know this doesn't make any sense, but it's starting to get dark, and I hate being in the cemetery after dark." As he spoke, he stood up from the modified golf cart and started shuffling from one leg to the other and rubbing the sleeves of his jacket as he tried to stay warm.

His coworker, Richard, was parked beside him sitting in a small bulldozer, often called a front-end loader, smoking a cigarette. He appeared unaffected by the biting cold weather. He looked over at Pete and shook his head in dismay. In a deep, scratchy voice damaged by at least fifty years of smoking a pack of cigarettes a day, Richard finally said, "Yeah, Father Odom is pretty long winded when it comes to funerals. And you're right. It doesn't make any sense that you are scared of the cemetery at night. You're an undertaker, for goodness' sakes!"

Both men were anxiously waiting for the priest to finish his graveside sermon and the small crowd to depart so they could bury the body and head out of the bitter cold weather.

"Lord, we commit this body to you and pray that…" the priest continued, but none of the members of the small crowd gathered around the oak casket was really listening. The fifteen or so people who braved the wet and cold Washington, DC, winter weather to pay their last respects to their family member, coworker, and friend were starting to wish they had departed with the larger group of mourners who attended only the church service and elected not to go to the grave site. No one anticipated the priest would conduct what was starting to become a brief service at the grave site, given the hour they just had spent in the chapel only a few moments ago.

"Father, we ask you to forgive this child of God, forgive all transgressions, forgive all sins and…" The biting cold wind blew through the bones of the attendees, but somehow it didn't seem to bother the priest as he kept a steady pace with his prayer. Another ten minutes passed before the group heard what they had been anxiously awaiting. "In the name of the Father, the Son, and the Holy Ghost…amen."

The Catholics in attendance and those who understand the tradition joined the priest in making the sign of the cross. As soon as he was finished, the group scattered and quickly made their way to their vehicles. They rubbed their hands, trying to warm them up and regain feelings in their fingers.

Father Odom waved his right hand in the air at the departing group and stated, "Peace be with you. Peace be with you." It was inconceivable that he could stand there with a broad smile in such bitter weather. Out of respect for the deceased, he stood by the grave site until the last vehicle departed. It was one of his traditions to stay with the body, to symbolize that their loved one was not alone, until the family and close friends left. Although he wasn't sure that anyone got what he was doing, he'd included that as part of this routine for so long, it had become a habit that he had no plans to change…even in bad weather.

It was just past 5:30 p.m. on a Friday afternoon in mid-November, and it was getting dark. Those standing in a cemetery in twenty-seven-degree weather with the wind howling as it blew past the ornate fixtures in this old cemetery created an eerie setting. The freezing rain only added to the misery, so no one felt ashamed about making a sudden exit once the priest had completed his prayer. The only one whom the weather didn't seem to bother was the person holding a shovel and standing in the distance among the trees. The dark trench coat against the backdrop of the trees was a camouflage that ensured the person could barely be seen. The individual stood motionless, straining to hear, but holding on to every word the priest uttered.

Pete and Richard waited for Father Odom to go past some of the larger structures in the cemetery. Once he was out of sight, they quickly converged on the site with their equipment and divided up the tasks so they could finish more quickly. Pete started loading the modified golf cart with the chairs and the Astroturf used to cover the ground around the casket. Richard immediately loaded the remaining odds and ends scattered around the casket. The large wreath on the casket was already frozen in place and took a little extra work to remove.

"I still don't think it's right, burying these folks in only a four-foot hole," Pete complained as he was loading the golf cart. "Something is just not right about that. We shouldn't be burying one body on top of another. That's just sacrilegious or something. Don't you think, Richard?"

Richard just ignored Pete's comment. He was focused on getting the job done so he could get out of the cold. Plus, he was getting tired of hearing Pete complain. Every time the weather was less than perfect, Richard could count on hearing Pete whine about something. Most of the times he just ignored him, but the added cold weather made Pete a bit more unbearable.

Richard had an idea. "Listen, Pete, why don't you drive the cart over to the chapel annex and drop off this stuff, and I'll lower the casket and finish burying the body by the time you return."

"OK, sounds good," Pete quickly replied. He knew going into the chapel annex would mean getting out of the cold. Even a few minutes of warmth would be a welcome change. So without a pause, he hopped into the golf cart and headed over to the annex next to the chapel.

As Pete departed, Richard worked on releasing the lock that kept the casket in place over the grave. Thanks to Father Odom's long sermon, the lock for the automatic casket-lowering system was frozen in place. Richard was so engrossed with fidgeting with the locking system that he didn't pay attention to the footsteps he heard approaching from behind. When the footsteps stopped, he turned to see who it was—just in time for his forehead to make contact with a shovel. The contact was so sudden and violent that it drove him backward, causing the back of his head to hit the frozen grass. He was barely conscious as he lay motionless and bleeding on the ground. He wanted to move but didn't have the wherewithal to do anything but lie there as he slowly drifted off into unconsciousness. He felt searing pain throughout his head and down his back. Blood trickled past his eyes as he watched in horror as the silhouette of a person struggled to remove the frozen body from the casket.

When Pete returned, a few minutes later, he found his coworker lying on the ground, barely alive, and the casket tipped over on its side. As Pete provided assistance, he used his cell phone to call for an ambulance. Pete initially assumed that the automatic lowering system had failed, causing the casket to topple and hit Richard in the head, but as he spoke to the 911 dispatcher, his eyes widened in shock as he noticed the casket was empty.

Chapter 1
COMA
(SEVEN MONTHS EARLIER)

"Oh my god! They almost hit us," screamed the SUV passenger as she watched the vehicles that had almost collided with them dodge in and out of the lanes ahead. A red Mitsubishi Evolution, better known as "Evo" by street racers, had just whipped around the corner at sixty-five miles per hour, fishtailing so much it almost went sideways. The driver, an experienced twenty-four-year-old street racer, slammed into third gear, pumped the clutch twice, and popped it as he floored the gas pedal. It was just enough to miss the blue Ford SUV and squeeze by on the left shoulder. Passing the SUV on the right after barely missing a taxicab was a silver Nissan 350Z.

"They're insane! They must be going a hundred miles an hour. They're going to kill someone racing around here like that!" the SUV driver responded, shaken by the near miss. Only seconds ago, the family had been cruising past the Pentagon on US Route 1, enjoying the excitement of passing such an impressive landmark. They were due to visit the Pentagon on Monday for their tour, and they were making sure they knew how to get there. But their relaxing family vacation and casual Sunday drive was briefly interrupted by two souped-up sports cars driving at breakneck speeds.

As the 350Z passed the SUV, it hit an oil spot and lost traction just as he gunned the gas. The driver pumped the clutch, hit the gas pedal, fishtailed for a few feet, and then straightened his car without giving an inch to his opponent. Both cars blasted alternative rock music so loudly they could barely hear the roars of their engines.

It was a beautiful spring Sunday morning, and the walking paths and sidewalks were filled with sightseers and joggers. In spite of the dangers to vehicles and pedestrians, these two friends heading home after a night of partying in DC and crashing at a friend's apartment decided to race toward a local café located off I-66 west. The prize for this madness was the loser had to pay for breakfast.

Both cars were zooming by Arlington Cemetery at seventy-plus miles per hour, swinging around vehicles like they were standing still. The Evo quickly swerved into the middle lane to get past a van only to end up behind a moving truck. He hit the brakes and downshifted into fourth gear to keep from rear-ending the truck. It was just enough of a pause for the Nissan to slip past both of them in the right lane then quickly switch back to the middle.

"Oh, hell no!" yelled the Evo driver as he swung into the far-right lane and hit his nitrous-oxide button, boosting the speed from seventy to ninety-five in fractions of a second. It was then that he realized he wasn't in a lane; he was on an exit ramp.

"Son of a—" The words had barely left his mouth as he realized he was in deep trouble. He was doing over 95 miles an hour and had only 150 feet to stop or somehow make a ninety-degree turn. The 350Z driver, not realizing his friend was in trouble, pushed his car even harder—105, 107, and climbing. He was bent on winning a free breakfast and bragging rights, a victory he could rub into his friend's face for weeks to come. His adrenaline flowed like water as he increased his speed and dodged around the few cars in front of him.

The Evo driver starting thinking, "This is going to freaking hurt" as he realized he didn't have enough road ahead to stop his car. He slammed on the brakes and jammed his car into third, completely skipping fourth gear. Everyone within a quarter mile heard the grinding of gears and the loud roar from the high-performance muffler system. The car swung to the left as it approached the intersection at the top of the exit ramp. He slammed it into second, hoping the compression would force it to slow down even more. That caused it to slide toward the small island and side-walk on the right, so he turned his wheel in the opposite direction while pulling up his hand brake as he tried to correct the slide. It was too little too late; the right front tire hit one of the many DC potholes, which sent the car jutting toward the left sidewalk. The nearby joggers and tourists who realized what was happening scrambled out of the way. There were several near misses as the car continued to slide. Within seconds, the car's left front tire hit the sidewalk, causing the tire to explode, sending the Evo airborne.

"Oh my god, oh my god," screamed the driver as he came to the real-ization he was probably going to die. The airborne vehicle seemed to move in slow motion as it inverted and headed toward Farid, a twenty-nine-year-old refugee from Syria who was simply standing on the other side of the bridge, looking through the hedges at the 350Z that was blasting through traffic at a hundred-plus miles per hour. He had heard the noise of the engines but thought it was coming from the 350Z, so he was caught up with watching the car on the road below him and didn't have any idea what was going on behind. The airflow of the car going sixty-five miles per hour caused a suction effect when it passed him, pulling him over the bridge with tremendous force. His jacket, which was in his hand, was sucked toward the car as it landed.

The family in the SUV and the taxi driver watched in horror as the car landed on the front bumper then flipped and spun into the air another hundred yards before plummeting into the thick overgrowth next to the road, some 150 yards from the bridge. It landed upside down and immedi-ately exploded into flames, igniting everything within twenty feet, includ-ing Farid's jacket and its contents—his wallet, cell phone, and ring of keys.

Between grabbing his jacket and the jet stream the Evo formed when it passed, Farid was literally pulled through the hedges, toppling head first over the side of Arlington Bridge. His arms and legs flung in every direction as he flipped like a rag doll. He heard a loud snap as he landed on his back, causing a hairline fracture in his neck and jarring his spine. The landing was so violent and the pain so excruciating that his body immediately went into shock, causing him to slip into unconsciousness in an instant.

The vehicle's explosion was heard throughout Arlington Cemetery as the nitrous oxide fueled the flames. Dozens of tourists ran away from the direction of the large blue plume of smoke fearing it was a terrorist attack. The drivers of the SUV and the taxi stopped and ran toward the vehicle to provide assistance, but it was already too late; the heat from the flames was just too great to allow them to assist the driver.

The driver of the 350Z had no idea what had just happened. He had already turned the corner and was on the entrance ramp toward I-66 west. Between his radio blaring and the loud noise from his car, he didn't hear the explosion. Besides, he was too focused on getting to the café first.

The woman from the SUV stayed with her kids but kept trying to get her husband's attention. She was trying to tell him about the man who had fallen over the bridge. He finally understood what she was saying, and he and the taxi driver ran over to Farid, who was lying unconscious on the top portion of grass leading up to the bridge. By the time they spotted him, they could hear the sirens of an ambulance and two fire trucks responding to the scene.

Within minutes of the explosion, officers from Arlington Cemetery and the Pentagon arrived on the scene and immediately cordoned off the area, blocked the road, and redirected traffic to the overpass. A sheriff and several local police officers arrived shortly afterward and joined in directing traffic away from the scene of the accident.

One of the officers noticed the two men on the hillside and went over to investigate. The two drivers were just finished checking on Farid when two paramedics arrived ready to assist.

"Over here! This man needs help!" yelled the police officer, and he waved to the ambulance driver to stop nearby.

The emergency technicians immediately took charge of the situation.

"He's still breathing. Do you think he'll be OK?" inquired the man from the SUV as he stepped out of the way to allow the technician to do his job.

The technicians ignored his question and immediately started to check Farid's vitals. They both noticed the gash that ran from the top right of his forehead to his left cheek. One technician quickly pulled out several gauze bandages, which he applied to the wound to stop the slow trickle of blood.

"What happened to him? Was he like this when you found him?" inquired one of the technicians.

"Yes. We just noticed him a minute or so before you showed up. Between my wife and me, we saw everything...everything," the SUV driver said, sounding a little louder than he expected. He made a conscious effort to speak a bit more calmly, but it was difficult after what he had just experienced.

"He was hit by the burning car from on top of the bridge, and he came tearing through those hedges. That's how he got that cut." This time his voice sounded a bit more normal. He was still a little fidgety as adrenaline flowed through his body.

One technician nodded, acknowledging that he had heard what the man said.

"Weak pulse and shallow breathing," one technician said to the other after he got the gauze in place. The lead technician immediately put an oxygen mask on him, mindful of the cut on his face. In the meantime, the other technician ran back to the ambulance and retrieved a neck brace and a separate back brace and started unraveling the straps.

"Can I help?" inquired the SUV driver.

"Thanks, we're good," replied the technician.

They took great care placing the neck brace on the unknown victim, ensuring they barely shifted his head to get everything in place. They were just as cautious as they slipped the fiberglass board under his back, as they made every effort to keep his body from shifting. Once the braces were in place, they strapped him securely to the board and then prepared to lift him on to the nearby stretcher. The two technicians struggled to get Farid up the grassy hill and to the back of the ambulance. Once there, they quickly pushed him into the back, secured the stretcher, and were on their way toward a nearby hospital.

The crews from the two fire trucks worked feverishly to put out the fire, but the nitrous oxide fueling the fire made it difficult to contain. The crews were concerned about the thick brush becoming engulfed in flames causing the fire to spread beyond the twenty-five-foot circle they were dealing with at the moment. After thirty minutes of working to put out the fire, they finally succeeded. The fire subsided.

The fire was so intense and the explosion so brutal that only a melted, twisted ball of metal and plastic remained. It was barely recognizable as once having been a car. The police officers stayed in the area and rounded up a group of potential witnesses to question. Against his wife's wishes, the SUV driver identified himself and his wife to the police as eyewitnesses to the entire incident and spent over an hour making statements before they were allowed to leave. The taxi driver followed the SUV driver's lead and stuck around to make a statement, although he knew it was costing him several fares.

It would be several hours before the coroner removed the driver's remains and the investigators had the vehicle moved to a downtown lot and stored as evidence.

On the way to the hospital, the ambulance driver radioed the dispatch. "We have a male, approximately thirty years old who fell from a bridge. Only visible injury is a laceration across his face, approximately six inches. He's unconscious and has a weak pulse. Given his position when we found him and the distance he fell, we suspect neck and back injuries. Our estimated time of arrival is five minutes. Over!"

"Got it. Unconscious male approximately thirty years old, with a facial laceration and suspected neck and back injuries. Arrival in five minutes," the dispatch responded.

"Roger," the driver replied and replaced the mic as he roared down the street toward the hospital.

By the time the ambulance reached the hospital, several doctors were awaiting its arrival, including a neurosurgeon, Dr. Zachary Gage. Dr. Gage had been paged by the head emergency-room nurse at the request of one of the emergency-room physicians who, after hearing the victim was unconscious, thought Dr. Gage's expertise would be needed if there were brain trauma.

Dr. Gage, Zach for short, is a brilliant, forty year old neurosurgeon who was currently in the last year of a five-year multimillion-dollar grant to determine how to bring victims back from trauma-induced comas. He'd worked on several patients whose families, after months of praying for a miracle, agreed to allow Dr. Gage to try his experimental treatments to revive them from their comatose condition. In two of the six cases, he saw improved brain activity with his treatments but had not succeeded in reviving anyone from a coma. He knew that two consistent problems he was dealing with were the age of his patients and their relatively poor health. The few young patients he experimented on were either too far gone to help due to multiple life-threatening injuries or their families were not ready to allow Dr. Gage to experiment on their loved ones until the individual's brain had deteriorated to the point where it was simply too late for him to make a difference. Dr. Gage was starting to get a bit desperate for suitable candidates, so he started spending more and more time keeping track of the patients coming into the hospital's emergency room. This time, when he was paged, he was eager to meet his prospective patient.

A thirty-year-old unconscious victim with a six-inch cut as the only visible injury was, potentially, Dr. Gage's perfect specimen. The ambulance arrived, and Farid was quickly triaged and found to be stable and breathing only slightly irregularly with forced oxygen. After a quick check by the attending physician with Dr. Gage by his side, the unknown patient was quickly wheeled to radiology to get a MRI on his upper torso, including his head, neck, and spine. Within thirty minutes, the doctors were able to determine that Farid had a hairline fracture in his neck and a slight hemorrhage in the lower left side of his brain. Dr. Gage quickly ushered him into surgery and was able to drain the clot and relieve the pressure that was slowly building in his cranium. Now stabilized, he was placed in the recovery room.

"So what do we know about this guy?" Dr. Gage asked the charge nurse who was going over his charts.

"Nothing. He didn't have any identification when he came in to the emergency room. I went through his clothes myself and found nothing, not even a set of keys. I expected to find a cell phone or at least keys. Isn't that strange?"

Dr. Gage was listening to the nurse, but he appeared preoccupied as he stared at Farid through the glass door. "Yeah, it is kind of strange. Have you made contact with the police yet to see if they found his wallet or keys or maybe even a report of a missing person?"

"Already did. The police said their investigators combed the area before they left the scene looking for evidence related to the accident. No wallet, no keys, and no missing person's report yet. But it's still too soon for the missing person's report. The police think in a day or so, someone will probably come looking for him," responded the nurse. "An officer is coming by later today to look through his things and to take some pictures and fingerprints to see if he comes up in their database. By tomorrow afternoon, his face will be all over the news, so his loved ones can come claim him."

"So what happens if no one comes forward in the next few days, and he doesn't come up in any database?" Dr. Gage asked. He knows the hospital has a protocol for dealing with John/Jane Doe patients; however, he had his own agenda and was hoping she would corroborate his thoughts as to what would happen next to the victim. Besides, he knew a scenario where no one came to claim him would be too good to be true.

"Oh, someone will be here to get him. He's a gorgeous man in great physical shape. I'm sure there's a girlfriend or two who will be here soon enough to claim him. Hell, if no one comes forward, I'll claim Frank. As soon as he comes out of that coma, I'll take him home," she said with a chuckle. "So do your magic on him, Doc. Do your magic and bring him out of that coma. A couple of us nurses already have dibs on him if no one shows up."

"Well, we'll see if I get to do any more work on him." The nurse calling the patient "Frank" had got Dr. Gage's attention enough for him to break his stare and turn and face the nurse. "Frank? How did you figure his name is Frank? I didn't think we knew anything about him." Dr. Gage seemed a bit bothered hearing the nurse call him Frank, thinking there was more to the unknown patient than the nurse was letting on.

"Oh, a couple of nurses and I nicknamed him Frank. He's too gorgeous to be a John Doe. He reminds us of a rugged and sculpted version of Ol' Blue Eyes, so we thought the name Frank suited him better. Don't you think?"

With that explanation, Dr. Gage visibly simmered down and continued his intense gaze at "Frank." He knew her reference to Ol' Blue Eyes was a reference to Frank Sinatra.

"Well, Nurse, you will have to get in line to claim our Frank," he said under his breath, not really wanting the nurse to hear what he said. Then he walked away and headed toward his boss's office.

Dr. Gage had a gleam in his eyes. He was desperate to find a suitable patient for his coma study, and right now, this new, unknown thirty-year-old "Frank" seemed to be a likely candidate. When he got to the office of the chief surgeon, Dr. Harry Emory, it was obvious he wasn't there. The mini blinds covering the glass door were drawn, the lights were off, and the door was locked. Dr. Gage suddenly remembered it was Sunday. He had been so focused on this new patient; he'd completely forgotten what day it was. He then looked at his phone and realized he had missed two calls from his wife. He'd been due home hours ago. He had promised to take his wife, the other Dr. Gage, to a play, and if he didn't leave now, he wouldn't make it on time. His plan would just have to wait until tomorrow.

Chapter 2
THE BETTER HALF

After a quick stop in the staff locker room to shower and change, Zach stopped by his office to retrieve his car keys and hang up his white coat. He was silently congratulating himself for having the foresight to bring his suit to work. He took one quick look in the mirror in his office to straighten his tie, grabbed his keys, and walked briskly to his car. As soon as he jumped into his car, he called his wife, Marcia.

"Hi, hon. Yes, I'm on my way. I'm already in the car and will be home in less than ten minutes. Yes, really, less than ten minutes." His voice changed a bit, indicating he was getting a little irritated. "Well, I'm sorry. I was just trying to save some random guy's life, that's all. Now I'm five minutes away. Are you ready? OK, that will work. I will just pick you up in the driveway, then. See you in a few minutes."

As exceptional as Zach is, equally brilliant is his wife, Marcia, an attractive thirty-nine-year-old neuroscientist. For the past two years, she had been working on a five-year grant to study the ability to regenerate brain cells that had been cryogenically frozen. The medical profession as a whole had had success regenerating virtually every organ in animals. However, regenerating brain tissue to its normal state, allowing specimens to be the same as before they were frozen, had been a real challenge. Marcia's studies had shown promise, but she was still having difficulties with full recovery of the brain cells in her specimens. In the meantime, she and her small staff continued to provide storage for the heads and bodies of the rich who paid the hospital significant sums of money to keep them frozen until a cure was found for their condition. Marcia was truly Zach's equal in every way and was equally driven when it came to her profession. She was just as determined as he to find the solution to regenerating brain tissue and cells to their normal state after they had been cryogenically frozen. But today was Sunday, and for now, she would be satisfied with Zach arriving home on time to take her to a play followed by dinner.

"Where is he?" she said out loud as she paced the driveway, limping slightly while looking down the street. Marcia was an avid runner, and a few years ago, she had been one of several casualties in a ten-person pileup in an Army 10K run in Washington, DC. It required a slight realignment of her lower spine and draining of several cubic centimeters of spinal fluid to relieve the pressure on her back. During the surgery, a small amount of cerebral fluid at the base of her skull was also removed for good measure.

As a research scientist, she had asked the surgeon just before she went in for surgery to save the vials of spinal fluid. She had no idea what she was going to do with frozen spinal fluid but figured she didn't want it discarded. The surgeon did as she asked and went one better by also saving half a vial of cerebral fluid he removed during the surgery. Marcia recovered quickly, and she was still able to compete in 10Ks and half marathons but no longer participated in full marathons. A combination of wear and tear on her body from years of running hundreds of miles combined with the accident and getting a little older (although she refused to admit age was slowing her down) caused her back pain on occasion. Also, when she became emotionally stressed or wore high heels for too long, she experienced a mild discomfort in her back that caused her to limp. It was so slight that most times she didn't even notice she was doing it.

After a couple minutes, she saw Zach's Volvo come around the corner and race toward her. It was obvious he was making a concerted effort to get there quickly. Marcia noticed this and calmed down a little. She knew Zach has an important job, but sometimes they both got too caught up in their work, so when they had free time, she was pretty jealous about sharing that time with anyone else, especially his job. She liked to use their limited free time to spend time together, doing things they both enjoyed. Tonight was a play and dinner, and up to this point, she had been pretty worked up about the prospect of being late.

They were both high achievers and fierce competitors in just about everything. With that, they also had a lot of passion for everything they did: work or play. Those very qualities that attracted them to each other were the same qualities that often caused friction in their four-year marriage. They gave a lot to each other in terms of emotional support, and they both demanded the same, so little things like being late for 'date night' because of work could quickly explode into an unnecessary argument.

As Zach approached the house, he noticed the slight limp and knew she was stressing. Her pumps were only a couple of inches high, so he didn't figure those were the problem today. Today it was his fault. He sped forward and pulled up next to the driveway with a screech. He jumped out of the car, gave her a nice kiss on her left cheek, said, "You look amazing," and opened the door.

"Now, that's more like it. Thanks!" she said with a smile. Zach knew he had to change her tone, or the night would be ruined. He'd used his phone to make reservations at a nearby restaurant and purchased tickets to the play online. The couple of minutes it took to complete these transactions between red lights really saved the evening. He'd forgotten about making the reservations until he was on his way home and just got lucky that the local play had been running for several weeks, and since it was a Sunday afternoon, there were still plenty of good seating options.

As promised, Zach was able to get them both there just before the play started; he was proud of himself for saving the day. After the play, they walked to a nearby restaurant, were ushered immediately to their seats, and enjoyed a fabulous dinner. Marcia even complimented Zach on his selection of seats at the play and the way they got seated at the restaurant immediately. He simply said, "Thanks." He dared not tell her he just had got lucky. It must really have been Zach's lucky day because they went home and had a great night of lovemaking and then went to bed. It took Zach a while to fall asleep as he lay there thinking intently about how he was going to get Frank as a patient in his coma-study program.

Chapter 3
DESPERATE MEASURES

The next morning, the Gages got up promptly at 6:00 a.m. to start their morning routine. After a nice, warm shower together, they had a quick breakfast of bran cereal and a shared banana; they kissed passionately in the garage and departed in separate vehicles, both heading to the hospital. They often left in separate vehicles because on any given day, it was too difficult to predict if Zach's schedule was going to get adjusted by some unforeseen emergency. It happened often enough that over time, they kept it simple by driving two vehicles. Because the hospital was only ten minutes away, driving the cars was not a burden on either one. They would take turns making a slight detour to stop by the gourmet coffee shop to pick up two cups of their favorite java. Today was Marcia's turn, which worked out perfectly for Zach, since he was anxious to get to the hospital and have a conversation with his boss, the chief of surgery, Dr. Harry Emory.

Zach arrived at the hospital in less than ten minutes. He looked in on Frank for a few minutes and then headed to his office to check if he'd got any e-mails or messages. He was anxious to talk to Dr. Emory about Frank, but as he approached Dr. Emory's office, he noticed it was still dark, indicating his boss wasn't there yet. For the moment, that was fine with Zach as he really didn't want to have the conversation until he downed at least half of his coffee. He returned to his office to follow up on paper-work and wait for Marcia before heading out on his rounds to check on the rest of his patients. As he looked at the digital wall clock, he figured

Marcia would be entering his office any minute. Within seconds, there was a sharp knock on the door. "Yes, come in," Zach said.

Marcia entered the office with her purse slung over her left shoulder and a large gourmet coffee in each hand. "Here's your coffee, Dr. Gage." Marcia smiled and curtsied in front of his desk. Zach smiled and took his coffee from her hand.

"Thanks. I need this before I go corner Harry about my new patient."

"What new patient?" Marcia inquired.

"The guy from the accident yesterday. Remember? The reason I was almost running late?"

"Oh, yeah, that new patient. So what's going on with him? Why do you need to talk to Harry about a patient you already have assigned to you?"

"I'm getting down to the wire on this grant, and I don't have anything substantial to report. At this rate, I won't be able to secure more funds for a follow-on study if I don't get to work on a patient who is not too old or has medical considerations that will contraindicate my treatment or will be too medically compromised to respond to the treatment. Frank is the best bet I have to fully implement my series of tests and medications to bring him back from a coma."

"So why ask Harry? What about just asking his family? I know Harry has to approve it after all the legal paperwork is resolved, but why start with him?"

"I'm sorry, Marcia. I haven't filled you in on Frank. He was in an accident that fractured his neck and gave a pretty good jolt to his spine. He showed up here without any identification so he is labeled—"

"John Doe," Marcia chimed in, indicating she was following the conversation.

"Anyway, the nurses decided to name him Frank because they think he looks like a fit and rugged version of a young Frank Sinatra."

Marcia looked at him sideways.

"I know, I know. I'm just going with it. What we call him is the least of my worries," Zach continued. "Bottom line, I want Harry to allow me to treat him with my experimental procedures if no one claims him in the next few days. I just need to show more progress in my treatments to secure another couple of million dollars to extend the study without going through the complete grant approval process. If I have to start from scratch, it's going to be an uphill battle."

Marcia knew there was nothing she could say or do to make the situation any better, so she just walked up and gave him a nice hug and ran her hand through his wavy brown hair. "You'll be all right, babe. You'll be all right." She paused briefly before letting out a sigh. "Babe, I'm sorry, but I've got to go." After a quick kiss on the top of his head, she slowly walked out as he watched her leave. She knew he was watching her so she took her time leaving and even swished a little so he could take in all the curves of her hips and buttocks. She figured what the hell. It would at least take his mind off his grant and Frank for a minute or two. She was right; Zach enjoyed looking at her. It reminded him of their lovemaking last night, and for a few seconds, he wasn't stressing about his grant.

Shortly after she left, Zach's mind came back to reality. He sat at his desk for another few minutes, taking large sips of the coffee and thinking through his approach to Dr. Emory. He knew he had to be convincing to get him to agree to conduct experimental work on a patient without consent from the patient or family. He knew he was a bit premature in asking the questions since it had been fewer than twenty-four hours since the accident, and it could take days or even weeks before someone came forward. The problem was Zach didn't have weeks to spare. He had learned in studying other patients that as each day went by, the patients sank deeper into a coma. There was a sweet spot of time where they could potentially cycle out of it, but it differed for each patient. Zach was convinced from his data that if he could start the treatment before the patient slipped into that deep, comatose state, he would have a 90 percent chance of reviving him. In Zach's mind, he needed to start the treatment right away.

After a few more sips of coffee, Zach decided it was time to go make his argument to conduct experimental treatments on Frank. As he walked down the hallway to Dr. Emory's office, he rehearsed what he planned to say in his head, complete with anticipated responses to Dr. Emory's protests and likely questions. As he approached, he noticed the lights were on and the office blinds were slightly opened, allowing Dr. Emory's silhouette to be visible.

Zach paused for a couple of seconds in front of the door before giving a heavy knock and walking in just as Dr. Emory instructed him to enter. "Hey, Zach, how are you doing?"

"Morning, Harry, I'm good. How about you?"

"Not bad. I had a quiet weekend, just spending time with the family. You and Marcia do anything special?"

"Yeah, we went out to a play and dinner. But anyway, listen. I wanted to talk to you about a patient who came in through the emergency room yesterday." Zach had been waiting to talk to Dr. Emory since yesterday and he had no time or patience for idle chat.

"What about this patient? Is there a problem?"

"No, he's our newest John Doe. He came in yesterday morning without any identification."

"Hang on, I was just going through the report from the charge nurse on surgeries we did over the weekend." Dr. Emory scrolled back through a report that was pulled up on his computer. "Are you talking about the thirty-or-so-year-old guy who's in a coma? The one you had to relieve the pressure on his brain due to slight hemorrhaging?"

"That's the one," Zach responded.

"OK, I'm with you now. So what's going on with this patient besides the fact that we don't know who he is?"

"Harry, we've got to start my series of treatments on him right away, or we'll miss our opportunity to revive him."

Dr. Emory opened his mouth to respond.

"Before you say anything, my meds are simply a cocktail of FDA-approved drugs combined in a way that will stimulate brain activity."

"Yeah, got it. But what about the little part about the electrodes also used to stimulate brain activity?"

17

"That treatment is also…" Zach paused for a second. "OK, well not approved by the FDA, but it is accepted in the profession."

"OK, hold up. Before we go off on that tangent, why would you think I would allow you to start these experimental treatments without the family's approval? We have enough lawsuits for legitimate treatments where we are completely in the right. I can't imagine the lawsuit for using an experimental treatment protocol when there are no extenuating circumstances. Are there extenuating circumstances, Zach?"

"Yes, there are. Two of them. As I showed you in the progress review last month, the reason why we haven't been fully successful in reviving coma patients is because we often start way too late. We start the treatment after the patient has slipped into a deeper phase of the coma. Starting the process early is the equivalent of waking a person just as he is dozing off instead of waiting until he is in a deep sleep or REM. It's a lot easier to wake him as he is dozing off."

"And the second?"

"This hospital will lose the grant, and I will not be able to get an extension, which is worth four to five million dollars over the next two years. Not to mention the additional funding the hospital will get when I succeed."

"*If* you succeed," Dr. Emory highlighted.

"I will succeed, but only if we start now, Harry. We must start now!"

"So if this goes badly, just how much do you think his family will sue us for—five million, ten million, more? That four or five million will be a drop in the bucket if this goes badly. Aaah! Zach, I want to support you, but damn it, we need to give it time for his relatives to show up and claim him. Then we can have this dialogue. This is too premature right now."

"You do realize—" Zach stopped midsentence. "Never mind. Is he still my patient?"

"Yes, he's officially a coma patient, and he's yours to care for."

"OK, thanks," Zach replied, a bit stiff lipped. He moved toward the door.

"Zach, don't do anything stupid. You have to wait. We have to wait."

"Got it." Zach stormed out the door and went to his office, where he slammed the door and started pacing.

"Damn it!" he exclaimed as he pounded his fist on his desk and knocked a couple of books to the floor. As he picked them up, he glanced at the wall clock and realized he was due to start his morning rounds. He quickly left his office and headed to check on his patients. The morning crept by as he thoroughly checked each patient and each chart. He spent extra time checking on his remaining coma patients, poring over their charts and his notes to see if there was something he'd missed that would have provided better results. After several hours of double- and triple-checking himself, he came to the same conclusion: nothing could substitute for starting the treatment early, *before* the patient slipped into a deep coma.

It was after 2:00 p.m. before Zach realized he was hungry because he'd missed lunch. He stopped by the hospital cafeteria, grabbed a sandwich and a coffee, and headed to his office, where he ate his lunch in the dark. He was in deep thought about Frank and what he should do. He still had not checked on him since early this morning and was having a hard time with Harry's insistence on waiting for Frank's relatives. As he finished the last bite of his sandwich, he took a long gulp of coffee and unlocked his cabinet in which he kept his experimental medicines to treat his coma patients. He removed a syringe and filled it with fifteen cubic centimeters of his concoction of medicines and headed to Frank's room.

Upon arriving at Frank's room, he found there was a nurse there checking his monitor and his vitals. She also seemed to be staring at him and was startled by Zach's entrance.

"Oh, hi, Dr. Gage," the nurse said with a slightly embarrassed look, realizing the doctor had probably caught her staring at the patient.

"Oh, hello," he responded, a bit off guard since he hadn't expected to see anyone in the room. "How's our patient doing?"

"He's doing fine. All his vitals are pretty much normal. From all the tests you ran yesterday, it seems as if he's as healthy as a horse—except he's in a coma and his neck has a hairline fracture."

"Yep, my thoughts exactly," Dr. Gage responded. Zach took a cursory look at his chart then checked his eyes using a flashlight. He noticed the whites of his eyes were starting to darken. He bit his lip in frustration, knowing that was the same phenomenon he noticed in his other patients as they slipped deeper into a coma. Each day for the first week of their coma, the whites of the patient's eyes would darken, and Zach would also notice a slowing of the blood flow in the brain. He knew he was fighting against time. He was desperate.

"Nurse...ahh, Johnson," he finally said after reading her name tag. "Would you mind giving him a sponge bath and changing his sheets. He went through quite a lot yesterday, and he could use another sponge bath."

"No problem, Doc!" the nurse responded, rather happy at the proposition of giving this handsome man a bath. "I'll get the supplies and sheets right away," she said and then quickly departed.

That was exactly what Zach was hoping for. As soon as she left the room, Zach pulled out his syringe and injected his concoction of medicine into Frank's IV. As the fluid entered Frank's body, Zach thought he saw him twitch for a brief second, so he stared at Frank, waiting to see it again. After a few minutes, Nurse Johnson returned with two other nurses, ready to change the sheets but also, more importantly to them, ready to give Frank a bath. Zach broke his gaze as they entered the room and then backed out of the room slowly as he watched the nurses work together to start giving Frank his sponge bath.

Zach went back to his office and plopped into his chair. He instinctively turned on his TV just to get his mind off what he just had done. The television was on a local news station that was covering the story about John Doe. "He's now called Frank by the hospital staff," the news reporter stated. They were saying that anyone who knew Frank should come forward as the hospital had no information on him. A phone number for a tip line appeared for a few seconds as the reporter transitioned to another story. Zach turned off the television, unlocked the right bottom drawer in his desk, and retrieved a small voice recorder that was nestled between several rows of mini cassettes labeled with names, numbers, and dates.

He removed the tape and replaced it with a new one, after writing the date and the name "Frank Doe" on the label. He then placed his elbow on his desk, which allowed him to hold the recorder a few inches away from his mouth, and started dictating. "Twenty-five April, Frank Doe, patient number thirteen. His name, age, date of birth, and where he's from are unknown. His age is estimated at thirty years old. Trauma-induced coma; approximately twenty-four hours since the incident. His blood work was normal. No indication of additional swelling of the brain. All seems to be healing nicely. I observed darkening of the whites of his eyes, consistent with my conclusion that the eyes darken as the patient slips deeper into a comatose state. I administered fifteen ccs of experimental drug CS1.

"I believe I observed a twitch when the drug was administered, but his movement is inconclusive at this time. It could have been simply an involuntary muscle spasm. I am confident he is the right candidate for the more aggressive series of treatments." Zach stopped the recorder, carefully placed it into the drawer, and locked it. It was now after 5:00 p.m., so he changed out of his scrubs. He was just about to lock his door behind him when his phone rang. After a brief pause where he contemplated whether to answer the phone, he finished locking the door and started to walk away. Little did he know, the next few seconds were about to have a significant impact on everything he had worked for all his life.

Chapter 4
CRISIS

He had taken only two steps away from the door when his cell phone rang and simultaneously he heard a page over the hospital's public-address system. "Code blue, code blue, two, two, six. Code blue, code blue, two, two, six." After a brief pause, the female voice announced, "Doctor Gage, please contact extension two, two, four, zero. Doctor Gage, please contact two, two, four, zero."

Zach knew exactly what the page meant: an emergency in room 226... Frank's room. Instead of calling the extension, he broke into a full sprint toward the stairwell halfway down the hall. Within a minute, he was in Frank's room and trying to catch his breath. Frank was having convulsions and throwing up green mucus and clear fluids. He was flanked by two nurses, who were holding his head over the side of the bed so that he could expel his fluids into a bedpan and not choke on his own vomit. One of the nurses stepped aside as Dr. Gage approached, allowing him room to examine the patient.

"How long has this been going on?" Zach asked the nurse holding the bedpan.

"It started just as I was approaching the room, maybe a couple of minutes ago. I noticed his body shaking, and as I walked in, he started vomiting," the nurse responded.

Another thirty seconds went by before Frank finally settled down, and the nurse rested his head on his pillow. Zach immediately started checking his eyes and his vital signs. He'd hoped that what he just witnessed was an indication that Frank was at least semiconscious. After checking his eyes, Zach realized that not only were his pupils not responding to the light, his eyes looked even darker. This was a clear indication that he was slipping even deeper into a coma. His vital signs were elevated but seemed to be lowering now that the situation was under control.

"Shit," Zach said under his breath when he realized Frank's condition seemed to have worsened.

"Who is the nurse in charge of this section tonight?"

"I am, Doctor," replied the nurse standing behind him.

"I need to go take care of something, but I'll be back in about fifteen minutes," Zach said. "Ensure someone stays with him until I return." He made a point of looking the nurse in the eyes as he continued. "Page me immediately if anything—and I mean anything—changes while I'm gone. I plan to spend the night, but I need to get a few things first."

"OK, Doctor. I'll have Annie stay with him." She motioned to the nurse standing by the door. "I need to get back to the desk."

"That's fine. I'll be right back, Annie."

Zach quickly retreated to his office and called Marcia. "Hi, honey. I have some really bad news. My patient Frank had an incident tonight that damn near killed him. Hell, it damn near killed me. He's all I've got to make this—" Suddenly, he realized what he was about to say. He did not have approval to start his experiments on Frank, and he was not about to tell Marcia what he did earlier, especially not while he was on the phone. "I've got to keep him alive so I can get approval to prove my theories."

Marcia held the phone away from her ear for a second and looked at it. She thought about how insensitive and selfish Zach sounded. She knew he was a good man, but right now it sounded as if his only motivation for keeping Frank alive was so he could use him as a guinea pig. Zach was so caught up in the moment that he didn't even think about how horrible he just had sounded.

"Anyway, I've got to stay here tonight. I've got to keep an eye on him."

"What do you mean, you have to stay the night?" Marcia inquired. "There are lots of other doctors and nurses on shift tonight. Why do you have to stay overnight with him?"

"I've got to make sure he's OK. I have to stay the night," Zach repeated.

"That's what the doctors on shift and the nurses are there for. Why do you have to stay the night?" Marcia repeated.

By now, Zach was starting to get agitated. He knew that Frank had probably had an allergic reaction to his experimental medication, but he could not admit to it...at least not now.

"Listen, Marcia, I'm sorry, but Frank is my last and only hope to keep my grant going. Remember, my grant expires in about a year, so I cannot afford to lose him. I'm simply not going to leave his life into the hands of just anyone who's on shift tonight. I'm sorry. I have to go check on him."

Marcia was upset and felt Zach sounded incredibly selfish. She did not want to deal with him right now and knew nothing she could say would make a difference, so she hung up the phone without saying another word.

"Marcia? Marcia?" Zach called into the phone before realizing she'd hung up.

He slammed the phone back on the receiver and pounded his hand on the table, giving out a loud and angry grunt. He grabbed the side of his head with both hands, tugging at his brown hair and yelling, "Shit, shit, shit!" He was really stressing about his grant and the possibility of losing Frank. Having Marcia hang up on him just added to his problems.

After a few seconds, Zach calmed down and went directly to the cabinet containing his selection of drugs. He removed four bottles and used a syringe to remove a couple of cubic centimeters from each. As he examined the syringe, the odd combination of medications swirled together turning an eerie light-yellow color. He stuck the syringe into his pocket and headed back to Frank's room. Zach was desperate, but he didn't realize at the time that this was only the beginning of his obsession with his patient.

Chapter 5
BREAKING POINT

Zach returned to Frank's room in time to see nurse Annie cleaning up the last of the mess Frank had made earlier. She turned as soon as he entered the room.

"Oh, hi, Dr. Gage."

Zach just smiled at her with his lips closed. "How is he doing?" Zach inquired.

"He's doing much better now. He's resting."

Zach looked at Frank's chart and started checking his feet and legs for any blood clots that might be forming. He checked his eyes, hoping for something astounding, but his miracle was a long way off given his assessment of Frank's situation. Although the full body check was necessary at some point, Zach was mostly doing it to seem occupied while he waited for the nurse to leave the room. Within a couple of minutes, Annie completed cleaning up and departed.

As soon as she departed, Zach pulled out his syringe and injected this new concoction into Frank's IV. He cautiously watched for a reaction, but there was nothing.

Zach then got comfortable in a nearby chair and sat there reading a few magazines and thinking about how horrible the conversation had been between him and Marcia. He was still thinking about what happened to Frank earlier as he dozed off to sleep.

The next morning, at 8:00 a.m., an eighteen-year-old man with a dirty rustic backpack walked into the hospital, went up to the information desk, and in very poor English said, "I here for my brodther."

"What?" asked the volunteer.

"My brodther. He on TV. He's here, yes?" the young man asked, looking nervous and uncomfortable.

As the volunteer tried to make sense of what he was saying, one of the nurses who had cleaned up Frank the night before was walking past on her way home from finishing her shift. She heard just the last couple of words, and it was enough for her to turn her gaze in his direction.

"Oh my God, oh my God! He looks just like Frank, just younger. Your brother is here. He's here." She looked at him for some sort of acknowledgment of what she had just said.

"Do you understand me?" she asked after a couple of seconds.

"Yes. My English is not very good, but I understand."

"Oh, good. I know someone who will be happy to see you. Stay right here," the nurse said as she pointed him to a chair. She then looked over at the volunteer and asked her to call Dr. Emory. "I'll go get Dr. Gage. He's in Frank's room."

The nurse took off quickly, and the volunteer immediately made attempts to reach Dr. Emory. After not reaching him on the phone, she tried his cell phone to no avail and paged him using the hospital's public-address system. Nabil was seated right below one of the speakers, and the volunteer's voice booming both over the speaker and fifteen feet from him startled him. He could tell there was a lot of excitement about him being there, and he was really starting to get nervous. Nabil had been in the States trying to reconnect with his estranged older brother after being separated in war-ravaged Syria. He really didn't have a connection with him, but after finding and corresponding with him on Facebook, he thought he should try to connect with him. With assistance from the organization in Germany that helped repatriate him there, he flew to the United States. He was required to purchase a round-trip ticket, and his flight out was today, and right now he was thankful he had that ticket in his backpack.

During the two weeks that he visited, Farid hadn't really paid much attention to him, so he had spent most of his time watching television. He came after being coaxed by one of his fellow refugees, who convinced him that since his brother was the only family he had, he needed to connect with him and establish a relationship. Unfortunately, connecting with his brother did not go as planned. Although Farid was happy to host him, he didn't change his routine during Nabil's visit. Farid disappeared overnight twice in the two weeks he visited, and Nabil later found out it was because he had spent a night or two with one of several girlfriends. Nabil was not interested in spending another day in the United States. He was ready to go back to his newly adopted home, and it was just by chance that he had caught the news report about his brother being in the hospital.

He and his brother were not close, and he'd always thought he was a bit of an ass. The past couple of weeks had just confirmed it. So when Farid went for a walk and a smoke a couple of days ago, the fact that he hadn't come back for a couple of days seemed normal. Nabil was starting to question why he even had come to the hospital. Right now, he was ready to leave.

As he looked around, he felt as though everyone was looking at him. It was as if every person passing by knew exactly what he was contemplating. The excitement of the volunteer now chatting on the phone with someone about him being there made him even more uncomfortable. As he looked around the hospital, he realized how nice it was, and he figured his brother was being well cared for. If he stayed, he might become responsible for him and possibly the hospital bills, and he was not in a position to take that on. The fact that he thought his brother was an ass just made the decision easier.

While the volunteer was distracted, he stood up and headed toward the door, trying to blend into a small group of people. Dr. Emory was just arriving as Nabil slipped into the crowd. He only caught a glimpse but immediately realized Nabil must be related to Frank.

"Hey, you there. Hold on a minute."

Nabil just walked faster and made a quick right turn as he exited the hospital.

"Hey, hold on," Dr. Emory yelled and doubled his pace. Within seconds he was at the door, but Nabil was nowhere in sight. Dr. Emory ran out to the parking lot, looking for a trace of where he had gone.

Just then the nurse was returning with Dr. Gage. They arrived just as Dr. Emory was jogging out the door. By the time Zach got to the door, he found Dr. Emory looking aimlessly around the parking lot.

"I freaking lost him," Dr. Emory said to Zach as he threw his hands into the air. "Where did he go so quickly? Why the hell would he take off?" By now the volunteer had gotten off the phone and had joined them at the door. "Did he say anything to you before he left?" an annoyed-looking Dr. Emory asked the volunteer.

"Ahh, no, nothing. He...he just left," she stammered. She knew she was busy talking on the phone and wasn't paying attention, so she felt a bit uncomfortable with the question.

"Damn it! I can't believe he just left. What did you say to him?"

"Nothing," the volunteer shot back quickly.

"Are you sure he was his brother?" Zach asked skeptically.

"I saw him for only a few seconds, but I would bet my paycheck that was his little brother," Dr. Emory replied. "Even from a distance, he looks just like John Doe—or Frank, as you call him."

"He said he was here for his brother," the volunteer chimed in.

This confirmation caused Dr. Emory to look at her with disdain. Suddenly, she wished she hadn't said anything.

As soon as he saw the trio of hospital staff walk back inside the building, Nabil emerged from his hiding place behind a white van and jogged to meet with the arriving bus at a nearby stop. He got on and headed to the airport, where he boarded a plane to Germany. His two-week trip to the United States to connect with his brother and to find a better life was a complete failure. Farid had been in the United States for more than two years. Nabil assumed he would be getting situated and would look for him and other family members who had been displaced by the war in Syria. What he found was that Farid was living in a small, grungy apartment and was spending most of his time with various women. Farid wanted no part of Nabil, and after the lack of assistance Nabil received, he planned to never return.

Ten hours later, Nabil landed in Germany and returned to the small room that he shared with a fellow refugee and friend. He told him the encounter with his brother had not gone well and that he never wanted to go back to the United States. Nabil never mentioned his brother's name again.

Chapter 6
CLOSING THE DEAL

"Nope, nothing to go on here. I can't see his face," the detective stated to Dr. Emory and Dr. Gage as they looked at the video recordings from earlier that morning. Dr. Emory asked Zach to come with him to the security office because he had spent the most time with their unidentified patient, and Dr. Emory figured he could help pick out the person the receptionist and the nurse said was a younger version of Frank.

"That tall guy pretty much blocked his face from the information center to the exit, and the information center's camera is out of focus," Dr. Emory observed as he looked at one of the hospital's security guards.

He got the message. "I'll get right on it, sir. OK, looks like we're done here. I appreciate you calling us, but without anything to go on, I'm sorry, but we can't go any further in this investigation. If anything else comes up..."

"Don't worry. We'll call," Dr. Emory finished up as he shook the detective's hand and escorted him to the door of the hospital's security room. "Damn it!" Dr. Emory exclaimed as he closed the door, almost slamming it. He looked around the small room for a moment as he showed the irritation on his face and said, "I'm going back to my office. Let me know if you need me for anything." He really wasn't speaking to anyone in particular; he was just making an announcement that he'd had enough of this issue for now. He was frustrated that he had a patient on one of his wards whom he knew nothing about. To add to his frustration, the only person who had come forward was now gone without any leads, thanks to the poor place-ment and obvious lack of attention to the hospital's security cameras. If the camera near the information counter had been in focus, they would have at least gotten a good view of the person and could have given the police something to go on. Of course, although he wouldn't admit it, Dr. Emory was very cognizant of the fact that this patient was costing the hospital thousands of dollars a day, and he had no idea how any of these bills would be paid. A coma patient could last weeks, months, and even years, and without the patient's identification, the hospital was unable to pursue pay-ment. That problem was not lost on Zach, so when he saw the opportunity to take advantage of the situation, he pounced on it.

"Hey, Dr. Emory, I'll walk you back to your office," Zach stated. Dr. Emory agreed with a nod, but he also looked suspiciously at Zach because he knew that the only time Zach called him "Dr. Emory" was when he wanted something, and he knew exactly what it was. After this morning's situation, he actually welcomed the discussion.

As they walked back to Dr. Emory's office, Zach made small talk about how it was a shame that so much time had passed and no one had come forward and how it was a shame that Frank wasn't getting the best pos-sible options for treatment because he didn't have anyone to make decisions for him or advocate on his behalf. Normally, Dr. Emory would have chal-lenged Zach on those statements by pointing out that as his doctor; it was his responsibility to provide his patient with the best possible treatment. But he knew where Zach was going with the conversation, and, although he'd already made up his mind, he thought he would just let him go through the process of trying to convince him to allow him to experiment on Frank.

As they approached Dr. Emory's office, Zach decided to focus on the fact that he was convinced would be the strongest point he could make to persuade Dr. Emory to allow him to experiment on Frank.

"You know; Frank's bill is costing this hospital close to two thousand dollars a day. Not to mention that he came in through our emergency room and was triaged and received emergency surgery to relieve the pres-sure on his brain. And let's not forget back and neck surgery."

By now they had arrived in Dr. Emory's office, and Zach was invited in to continue the conversation.

"So, you know if he were a patient in my coma research, the grant could pay for his treatment and—"

"All right, I got it. The answer is yes," Dr. Emory finally said in obvious frustration.

"I'm sorry, I didn't catch that. Did you just say yes? I can add him as a research patient?"

"Yes, that's fine. Technically, it's much too soon to make this decision, but let me get with the hospital's board of trustees and lawyers. This issue with his so-called brother showing up and disappearing this morning might give us the legal angle that he appears to be abandoned. Under conditions of abandonment, the hospital is generally granted the right to make decisions on behalf of the patient. In this case, your experimental treatment would be in the best interest of our patient, giving him the optimum chance to recover. It is in his best interest, isn't it, Zach?"

"Of course it is," Zach replied sharply.

"You can plan to start his treatment regimen in the morning. If the lawyers have any issues, I'll let you know. You'll need to keep accurate records in case we get sued by him or his family down the road."

"Got it. I always do," Zach replied as he departed and headed toward his office.

He was glad to get the news. He knew he'd already started experimenting on Frank, but with Dr. Emory's approval, he could now do virtually everything he felt was necessary in the name of research, and he wouldn't have to hide it as he had the past twenty-four hours.

Zach entered his office and locked the door. He went directly to where he kept his recorder and replaced the cassette with a new one. As he started his dictation, he systematically pulled the tape out of the hard cassette shell and cut it into pieces. "Twenty-six April, Frank Doe, patient number thirteen. His name, age, date of birth, and where he's from are unknown. His age is estimated at thirty years old. Trauma-induced coma; approximately forty-eight hours since his incident. His X-rays and blood work all normal. No indication of additional swelling of the brain. His back and neck surgery went well, and, according to the notes from Dr. Soto, the attending orthopedic surgeon, all seems to be healing nicely. I observed darkening of the whites of his eyes, consistent with my conclusion that the eyes darken as the patient slips deeper into a comatose state. I will administer fifteen cubic centimeters of experimental drug CS1 in an attempt to stop him from slipping into a deeper coma and will monitor his progress."

Zach turned off his recorder, tossed half the spool of tape he cut in the trash, and kept the other half to be thrown away somewhere else. He changed his clothes, took a deep breath and then exited his office. There was no need to check on Frank; he had already spent the night in his room. Besides, he would be back later tonight. Right now he had to focus on how to make up with Marcia.

Chapter 7
TURNING POINT

On the way home, it finally hit him that Marcia was at work. "Wow, she must be really pissed," he thought. "She didn't even drop by with a cup of coffee. I suppose I have some serious making up to do." He hadn't slept well the night before, as he'd gotten up several times to check on Frank. He was feeling tired, but he knew he had to take care of a few things before getting any rest. First stop was the florist, where he ordered a dozen roses to be delivered to Marcia at work. He enclosed a short note telling her he was sorry and wanted a chance to make it up to her. While waiting to complete his order, he used his phone to make dinner reservations at her favorite restaurant. "Mission complete, for now," he thought, then headed home to get some rest.

He had been asleep for only a couple of hours when the phone rang. "Hello," he said, still groggy.

"Hi, Dr. Gage, I know you're resting, but the instructions in Frank's chart indicate I'm to call you whenever something happens with him." That got his attention, causing him to suddenly sit up in bed.

"What about Frank? What's wrong?"

"He's doing fine now, but he was having convulsions for several minutes. Dr. Emory was called in, and since then, Frank has settled down. He's doing—"

"I'm on my way," Zach interrupted. He jumped out of bed, brushed his teeth while he showered, and was out the door in less than fifteen minutes.

It took him another seven to arrive at the hospital and dart toward Frank's room. Upon arrival, he saw him peacefully resting as he'd left him a few hours ago. After doing a check of his vital signs, he ordered more lab work. This time he logged his request against the grant funds in anticipation of Dr. Emory doing his part with the necessary legal paperwork. He knew the results would be back in a several hours, which allowed him the opportunity to check on his other patients.

By late evening, the lab results were available, but, unfortunately, they didn't give him any indication of what might be the problem. He spent the rest of the evening reading through articles and research conducted on coma patients, hoping to find something he might have overlooked. He still had not spoken with Marcia, and he completely forgot about their dinner reservations.

It wasn't until he was leaving the hospital at 9:00 p.m., when he saw a bouquet of flowers at the information desk that he realized how much he had messed up his opportunity to make up with her. Zach was tired, and he just didn't care at the moment. He just wanted to go home and sleep. He didn't notice that the note on the flowers was in his handwriting. When Zach got home, Marcia was already in bed, so making up at that point was not an option.

He assumed she'd gotten the flowers; unfortunately for him, that was a bad assumption. By the time the delivery person had arrived at the hospital, Marcia had already left for the day, so the receptionist decided to keep them on her desk and have them delivered in the morning. Zach went to bed assuming that Marcia was still upset with him in spite of the sincere apology he wrote in the note and the bouquet of flowers he had had delivered. Feeling the cold shoulder, he decided to leave her alone. That assumption was the starting point of what would become a serious rift in their relationship.

Chapter 8
PATCHING THE RELATIONSHIP

Over seven months went by, and Zach had fully dedicated his time to Frank. Frank became the subject of the most intense and advanced procedures designed to awaken him from his deep coma. There were a couple of occasions where his brain activity increased, and the whites of his eyes were less dark, indicating a better flow of blood to the brain and leading Zach to feel he was on the right path to recovery, but then Frank would end up in an even deeper stage of coma a few days later.

These rays of hope leading to disappointment put Zach on a mental roller-coaster ride for several months. His relationship with Marcia suffered due to the stress he was under; Frank would show signs of progress only to later regress, which conversely caused Zach to spend more time with Frank, trying to figure out what went wrong. Marcia, feeling neglected, also buried herself in her research on bringing mammals back to life after cryogenically freezing them for weeks at a time. She had accomplished a 99 percent success rate in bringing lab rats back to life after freezing them and was now ready to experiment on larger animals. She succeeded on a young pig that survived for a couple of days, only to die after continually slamming his head against the cage until he got a blood clot in his brain and died.

After that incident, Marcia took a couple of days off from work, which gave her time to think about the quality of her and Zach's relationship. With Zach's obsession with Frank, and Marcia burying herself into her work, they both didn't realize they had worked through the summer and fall without taking their usual vacations. It had finally gotten to a breaking point, so on her second day off, during which she did nothing but sit at home and brood, she got dressed and met Zach at this office.

"Zach, we've got to talk."

"I know, I know," Zach agreed while holding his head down.

"Listen, Zach, over the last seven months, I barely know who you were. We haven't spoken more than a couple of words to each other, and as for making love, that's been months. I know you are consumed by this project but—"

"Frank is not a project," Zach interrupted while looking down. He wanted to make up with Marcia, but he'd gotten very close to Frank and didn't want him insulted. "He's a living, breathing human being," he continued.

"OK," Marcia replied, not sure how to respond to what Zach had just said. As she replied, Zach caught the hint he had only put Marcia more on edge, so he quickly apologized.

"Marcia, right now, I feel as if my life's work is lying in the palm of Frank's hand. If I can just figure this out, it would make all the difference in the world. Look, I'm making progress." He handed Marcia a stack of Frank's records. Marcia gave the charts a cursory look just to satisfy Zach.

"Look, I can't speak to how well Frank is doing, but I can tell you we are doing horrible as a married couple."

"Fair enough. How about I cut out of work early today, and we go have a nice early dinner and talk more," Zach said from out of the blue.

Marcia wasn't prepared for that response, so she paused for a minute and just stared at Zach as she pondered the answer she should give him.

"OK. That's a good start. You know the routine for when we go out."

"Yep, I got it," Zach replied.

"I'll leave so you can get back to work and finish up early." Marcia walked up to Zach and pecked him on the cheek, something she hadn't done in a long time. As she touched his chin and the rough beginnings of a beard, she realized how old he looked. They had not been intimate for a while, and for long days, they mostly passed each other in the house. She figured with both of them slipping into poor diets and long days, the stress of their jobs was taking a toll, but she simply didn't realize just how much until this very moment.

After the quick peck, Marcia left and went home to get ready for dinner. True to his word, Zach stuck around long enough to do his final rounds of several patients and finished with checking on Frank, which he followed by a quick status dictation on his recorder about Frank's condition.

"No significant changes to condition. He seems stable and does not appear to be slipping any deeper into a coma. Will continue with current combination of medicines and increase by another ten cubic centimeters. Tomorrow, I will increase the frequency of shock—scratch that, electronic brain stimulation—treatments."

He didn't know it at the time, but that was the last time he would see Frank alive.

Chapter 9
GOING, GOING, GONE

Zach and Marcia had a pleasant dinner followed by light cocktails, so by the time they arrived home, they were both feeling rather friendly toward each other.

"Zach, instead of sleeping in the guest room, why not just come to bed?" Marcia asked with an inviting look.

"Sure!" replied Zach, immediately taking off his shirt on his way to the bedroom. By the time he followed Marcia to the room, she was already in the bathroom changing. Zach got excited and removed the rest of his clothes, anticipating her appearing wearing a set of his favorite lingerie. To say he was disappointed would be an understatement. She returned wearing a set of long pajamas.

"You need to put that thing away," she said, pointing at his manhood. "Just because you took me to dinner and we are getting along again doesn't mean all is forgiven after seven months of being basically roommates," Marcia said in a coy tone. She actually really wanted him but resisted the urge. She wanted to make sure that tonight wasn't just a quick "fix" for both of them, only to see him go back to dedicating practically every waking hour to studying Frank.

"Are you kidding me?" Zach replied. "Come on, don't do that," he pleaded.

"Sorry, not tonight. We need to work through some more of our issues before we get back to that point," she replied and kissed him on the cheek before crawling into bed.

"I thought that's what we were doing tonight at dinner...working through our issues."

By now she was under the covers, ignoring him. He knew the conversation was going nowhere, so he lumbered to the bathroom, dressed in a pair of long pajama bottoms and a T-shirt, brushed his teeth, and lay beside her.

"Please hold me," Marcia requested. Zach looked at her; he was puzzled for a few seconds, and then figured, why not. He held her in his arms, and they both fell asleep.

By the time, Zach got up he smelled a strong brew of coffee. Marcia had gotten up early and was using her newly purchased flavored coffeemaker, which made individual cups of coffee.

"Wow, that smells wonderful. What is that?" Zach inquired.

Marcia smiled. "I thought it would get you up. I'm having caramel with cinnamon and yours is French vanilla."

"Awesome. I hope it tastes as good as it smells."

After enjoying their coffee, they took turns showering and getting ready for work. The dinner, wine, and cuddling time last night had broken the icy treatment they'd given each other for months. Although Marcia wasn't going to give in to Zach's sexual advances for at least a few days, she didn't mind him admiring her as she took her shower while he shaved. She even intentionally walked naked from the shower over to the linen closet to get a towel to dry off. Things were starting to seem like normal as they smiled at each other. Then suddenly Zach's cell phone started ringing. He looked at the number and realized it was the hospital.

"Dr. Gage," he answered.

"Zach, it's Harry Emory. You really need to get here quickly."

"Is it Frank?" Zach asked excitedly into the phone.

"Just get here as fast as you can!"

Zach and Marcia quickly dressed, and Marcia insisted on driving to the hospital for fear that Zach would travel at such breakneck speeds that he would get into an accident and land them both in the hospital.

"What room is Frank in?" Marcia asked.

"He's in room two twenty-six."

"OK, I'll meet you there."

Marcia raced to the hospital but was very careful not to speed through the two camera speed traps along the way. She dropped Zach off in the front entrance of the hospital and watched him jog in before pulling off to park in her reserved spot. Within a few minutes, she was approaching Frank's room, only to see Zach speaking with Harry in the hallway just outside the room. Zach was staring blindly into the room, and Harry had his hand on his shoulder as he talked to him. As Marcia walked up, she arrived in time to get a glimpse of Frank before the attending physician, Dr. Morris, pulled the sheet over his head. Harry and Marcia nodded at each other in acknowledgment, and Marcia hugged Zach and said, "Oh baby, I'm so sorry. I'm so sorry."

"Marcia, why don't you just take Zach home? I'll have someone cover his rounds for today."

"Thanks, Harry. I'm fine. I'm better off at work. Let me wash up a bit and get my coat, and I'll start my rounds."

Dr. Emory knew Zach was right. He was better off keeping busy at work, so he nodded in approval and walked away slowly. Marcia accompanied Zach to his office and waited there until he returned from the men's locker room dressed in his scrubs. After he returned to the office, she removed his lab coat from his cabinet and helped him put it on. She sat with him for a few minutes.

"Marcia, I know you have work to do. I'm fine...really."

Marcia stared at him, trying to read his body language. "You sure you don't want me to stick around for a while longer?"

"No, I'm sure. I'll be fine. I just need to make sure I don't lose my other patients. It's best that I stay busy, or I'll just sit here or at home getting pissed off."

"OK, I understand. But I'll be back for lunch around noon…no excuses." Marcia looked directly at Zach as she spoke, hoping for positive acknowledgment.

He glanced up at her and nodded. "OK."

"Plan your day so we can both leave at four thirty and not a minute later." Again, she stared at him, waiting for his response.

Again he nodded and said, "That sounds good." He forced a half smile as he responded.

Marcia knew she was breaking through to him a little, so she pushed him a bit. "Come on, Zach. That didn't sound like a commitment to me. Four thirty, right?"

"OK," he said quietly.

"You know the words I'm looking for," Marcia continued.

"All right. Deal," he finally replied after a brief pause, this time giving her a full smile.

Marcia strolled over and kissed him on his cheek and headed to the basement lab where she did her work. "See you at noon," she said on her way out.

Zach just smiled and started to dig into his drawers for the files belonging to his patients.

On the way to her office, Marcia came across Ed, an orderly pushing a gurney with a body.

"Hey, Ed. Who's that?" she inquired.

"The guy never had a name. The paperwork just has John Doe, and next to that is the name Frank."

Marcia tilted her head to the side, indicating she was thinking. "Um, that's the guy that I'm supposed to have donated to my lab."

Ed stopped for a moment and looked at the paperwork.

"Dr. Gage, it doesn't say that on his paperwork. I'm just supposed to get him to refrigeration in the morgue and wait for the coroner's office to pick him up."

"OK, Ed. That's because there's a mix-up with the paperwork. Tell you what. I'll sign for him so he doesn't get lost in the system, and I'll follow up with the administration office and straighten it out."

"Well, if you sign for him, he becomes your responsibility. You realize that, right, Doc?"

"No problem, he's supposed to come to my lab. I'll gladly sign for him."

"OK, Doc. Sign right here, and he's all yours."

As Marcia signed the paperwork, Ed asked, "So where do you want him?"

"Oh, just follow me. I'll take him to the cryogenics center." Ed followed Marcia down several winding hallways until she got to a door where she had to swipe her badge and enter a four-digit code.

"Hey, Doc, I thought your team moved from this old section of the hospital to a newly renovated area just down the hallway."

Marcia knew Ed was right. She was taking Frank to the old work center, which wasn't being used anymore. She knew she couldn't take him to her current lab, because she would have to explain to her team why she had this stolen body.

"That's right, Ed. We work in the new lab just down the hallway. But we still use this section for storage of our research and development. Since he is donated to us for research and development, we'll just store him down here." After getting a question like that, Marcia knew she definitely did not want Ed in the old lab. "Thanks, Ed, I got him from here," Marcia said and took possession of the gurney.

Ed tried to look into the room, but Marcia deliberately blocked his view with her body as she wheeled Frank into the room. She quickly closed the door and leaned against it as she caught her breath.

"Now what?" she thought as she stood there looking at the shape of the body under the white sheet. After several long seconds, she realized she had to work quickly. She removed the sheet and paused as she thought, "So you are the SOB who took my husband from me for the last seven months. You bastard. How could you die on him? He dedicated so much to you, and you just died."

She was speaking out loud but didn't realize it for a few seconds. While she spoke, she quickly worked to get the equipment set up to cryogenically freeze him. Within minutes, the process was started. An hour later, she cleaned up the area and wheeled him into storage and tagged him as "John Doe, research cadaver."

As she left the old lab, she secured the door and paused. "What am I doing? What the hell am I doing?" She wasn't sure why she had taken Frank's body. As she walked toward the main section of the Cryogenics Research and Development Center, she was going through a wide range of emotions—angry that he died after Zach had dedicated so many months caring for him, jealous that he had taken so many months away from her and Zach, and excited because she was going to vindicate Zach's work by experimenting on him. Beads of sweat were still on her brow when she arrived at her work center. She got there thirty minutes late for the morning meeting with her team.

Although she was late, the meeting started as normal with Marcia asking the team about the status of their assigned projects and communicating pertinent information either from the hospital senior staff or providing guidance about where she would like to see progress. Suddenly, Marcia stopped in the middle of a sentence and seemed to drift off for a few seconds.

"Doc, are you OK?" asked her assistant, Angie, one member of her eight-person team.

"Huh. Oh, yeah. I mean, of course," Marcia responded slowly.

"You just look a bit flushed, and you just stopped in the middle of a sentence. You're not getting sick, are you? And why were you late this morning?" Angie inquired.

"No. I'm fine." Angie's questions irritated her a little, but she knew this wasn't the time or place to get into an argument with her, so she just ignored Angie's question about being late. "Listen, enough talking. We have a lot to do, so let's get to work." She ended the meeting and went to the restroom that was at the far end of the exterior hallway instead of the one within the lab section. She just needed time to think.

She'd taken possession of Frank's body mostly out of anger and hadn't really thought through what she was going to do. Although she mostly had kept her composure at the staff meeting, her mind was racing. She knew if what she did was discovered, she could lose her job, but she was now committed, and there was no turning back. The problem was, she was committed to what? She wasn't ready to answer that question to herself. She washed her face, looked at herself in the mirror, and took a deep breath.

"I guess you're committed now," she said to herself. She put on her best poker face and returned to her office in the lab and started going through some paperwork. She contacted Bob at the coroner's office and told him there was no need to retrieve John Doe because a decision had been made to donate his body to science. Because she had worked with Bob numerous times dealing with bodies that were donated to science, he didn't question her. As far as the hospital administration was concerned, John Doe was off their books. Marcia knew she was clear to do whatever she wanted with Frank, and no one would know any difference.

Lunchtime arrived quickly, and, as agreed, Marcia tracked down Zach doing his rounds and politely asked him to join her for lunch in the hospital cafeteria. As they sat there making small talk, Marcia realized this was a good time to guide the conversation toward her getting her hands on Frank's files. So as lunch ended, she innocently asked, "Hey, hon. I know this has been hard on you. How about I come back to the office with you and help you file Frank's paperwork."

"Well, I still need to go through Dr. Morris' report. He was the physician who tried to resuscitate him when he coded this morning."

Marcia reached for Zach's hands from across the table. "Zach, you did all you could. Please, for your sake—for our sake—just let it go. I know you have everything on your tapes. Let's just pack up his records for archiving and move forward. We've lost months and months of quality time, and our marriage has been strained. Can we just close this chapter and move forward?"

Marcia meant what she was saying, but her motive behind the words was simply to get her hands on Zach's records on Frank.

Zach knew she was right, but he really wanted to know what had gone wrong and caused Frank to die. Was it something he did wrong, something he had missed? He looked at Marcia's pleading eyes and realized he was better off leaving the situation alone for now and just agreeing with her.

"OK, let's go pack up his records and get out of here early, like you said. What do you say?" Zach said as he forced a smile.

Marcia returned the smile and said, "That sounds wonderful...deal." They got up and dumped their cups and paper plates in the trash, placed their trays on the shelf next to the trash can, and headed toward Zach's office. On the way, they stopped by one of the supply closets and found a box with a couple of reams of paper. Marcia placed the reams of paper on the shelf and took the box, several folder dividers, and some black permanent markers to Zach's office.

"These should come in handy," she said as she closed the closet door and continued toward Zach's office.

Marcia labeled and placed the dividers in the box to separate the various categories of the records. As she loaded the records, she paid particular attention to the results of all his lab work. "So what's this?" she would ask periodically as he handed her files from his cabinet to place into the box. After the third time, he just got into the routine of stating what the stack of papers contained.

"You know; I should really keep these records. They are part of my research. I still must report to the board that funds—or should I say, funded—my research since the grant money is about five months from being depleted. Damn it, I have no documented success to convince them to grant me an extension or renew my grant. This really stinks. My life's work is going down the drain."

Zach's shoulders drooped, and he looked like a defeated man. Marcia rubbed his shoulders and tried to console him the best she could, given her own dilemma.

She did feel sorry for Zach, but she was also a bit angry at him for basically abandoning her for all those months. Still, she knew this wasn't the time to deal with anger. She really wanted to be there for him, and she wanted a chance to put Frank through some of the most experimental procedures she knew. Her suppressed anger had taken the place of her compassion—so she continued to scheme.

"Hon, it will be all right. I'll tell you what. Instead of taking this box to the record archive section, how about I store it in my office? I have plenty of room, and it will free up your office to file all the other records you have all over the place."

Marcia looked around the office and pointed to several stacks of records that were tucked neatly on the floor. Her point was well made.

"OK, fine. Let's move these down to your office, and I'll file these records later. At least now I will have more room. I guess I was so focused on our Frank that I took the time to keep only his records properly filed."

At this comment, Marcia smiled and helped Zach finish clearing out his records on Frank.

"OK, that's the last one," Zach said after handing Marcia another file.

In a flash, Marcia removed her keys from her pocket, detached her office keys, and tossed the car keys to Zach. "I'll take this down to my office while you let Dr. Emory know we are taking a personal half day. I'll meet you by the basement exit."

Zach paused for a second, intending to say the box was too heavy, but Marcia was already headed to the door before he could get a word out. The box was a bit heavy for her, but she now had her hands on all of Frank's records. She planned on studying them and getting detailed knowledge on the results of every test. She had to know his medical problems so she could compensate for them and bring him back to life.

Marcia reached her office in record time but decided to place the box in the abandoned work center. The lab had downsized over the years, and the hospital simply moved everyone into a renovated section and closed off the area that was no longer being used. That's where she stored Frank.

Marcia swiped her card, entered her PIN, and went into the room. She quickly stored the box in what used to be her office and took a quick glance at where she had placed Frank's body. Her adrenaline was flowing, and she was starting to sweat again. She ensured the door locked behind her as she entered the outer hallway door and made her way to the exit. In seconds, she was outside and hopped into the car with Zach.

Chapter 10
THE EXPERIMENTS

Zach and Marcia went home and had great sex. They had not been to-gether like this for months. Marcia initially tried to play hard to get, as she was still holding on to some anger, but she really missed Zach's touch, and she always enjoyed sex with Zach. To Marcia's best recollection, their last meaningful sexual encounter had been at least a week before Zach decided to spend the night at the hospital after Frank had his first major medical scare. It had been months.

"Oh, my gosh, I really needed that, Marcia. You have no idea how much. I was really tense. I'm sorry. I put my work ahead of our relationship."

"Zach, I needed you, too. I'm sorry I let this drag on for so long. I guess we are both to blame...mostly you, though."

Zach knew she was poking fun, but he also knew she was right. "I won't argue with that. Let's not let our egos and work tear apart our rela-tionship. Deal?"

Zach paused, waiting for Marcia to respond. She purposely delayed so that Zach would sweat for a few more seconds, knowing most of the fric-tion between them was his fault.

"Yes, deal," she finally said in a sweet tone and hugged him. "Hey, this is the first time we've been off this early in a while. Let's take a shower and go shopping," Marcia said in a jovial tone.

Zach was thinking he would prefer a nap but realized he needed to be accommodating. "OK, I'm in."

Marcia hadn't actually expected him to agree with her. They had known each other since college, and she knew that after sex, all Zach wanted to do was sleep. She knew he was just agreeing to stay on her good side given the tension in their relationship for the past several months.

"I tell you what. I know you'd prefer to sleep. Why don't I just shower and pick up a couple of things I need at the mall. I'll pick up something for dinner and a movie for tonight."

Zach couldn't believe his ears. That was an irresistible offer. First, he got great sex, which he hadn't gotten for months, and now he actually got to take a much-needed nap.

"Wow, that sounds great." He paused for a moment, thinking she was setting him up for something or just testing him to see his response. "Wait, are you sure you want to go by yourself, or are you just testing me?" Zach asked.

"Absolutely, babe. You've had a lot of stress lately. You can stay and rest. I'm good with you not coming."

Marcia got up and ran to the shower. By the time she was finished and dressed, Zach was already dozing off. She jumped into her car and instead of turning left toward the mall, she turned right and headed straight for the hospital.

As soon as she got there, she removed her employee parking decal from the rearview mirror and parked in the patient parking back lot, not far from the basement entrance where Zach had picked her up several hours ago. She quickly slipped in and went straight to the old work center. She was able to avoid the main lab and was careful not to be seen, or so she thought. Her assistant, Angie, was just coming out of the restroom and saw Marcia enter the abandoned lab. She thought it odd and was about to inquire when a coworker standing in the doorway to the main lab yelled, "Angie, come quickly. I want to show you something."

"OK, I'm coming." Angie kept looking back as she returned to the lab. Marcia heard the brief conversation and suddenly wondered if she had been discovered. She paused for a moment, waiting to hear the door close before heading to her old office. She used the penlight she kept on her key ring to see where she was going until she got to the office, where she turned on the light.

She knew exactly what she was looking for. She'd carefully labeled the records in sections so it was easy for her to find his lab results. She spent almost an hour poring through his lab results and some of the cryptic notes from attending physicians who wrote in his chart when they checked on him during the very few times that Zach was away from the hospital.

She knew reading his records could have waited, but she was so excited about the prospects of experimenting on a human, she just had to start the process of getting smart about his health history. She knew that for her work to be effective, she had to know what he had been exposed to in Zach's research and how he had reacted. Plus, she was interested in seeing if his heart was strong enough to withstand the punishment she was going to put it through when she thawed him out. Suddenly, she looked at her watch.

"Oh my goodness. I better get back." She had been gone for almost an hour. She knew she could count on Zach napping for at least an hour and a half, but she still had to pick up dinner and account for her time shopping at the nearby mall. She quickly and quietly locked up her old office and the outer door, exited the building, and jogged to her car.

As she entered the car, she immediately removed her phone from her purse and touched the icon for a nearby Chinese restaurant. She was so used to ordering from that restaurant that she had completed her online order before she left the parking lot. Realizing she needed to show that she had gone shopping, she drove at breakneck speed to arrive at the restaurant within minutes.

She knew Zach would start to get curious or sense she was hiding something if she showed up without something from the store. She needed something...anything. Zach knew she never came home from the mall empty-handed...never. She was still trying to figure out what to do about a quick purchase as she opened the trunk to place the food. She had a plastic trunk liner and a perfect bin in which to put the food to ensure that if the soup spilled, it would be in the plastic bin and not on the BMW's carpet.

As she opened the trunk she saw a bag that contained a brand-new pair of running shoes she had bought a couple of weeks ago. She smiled. "Perfect. Now I have a reason why I've been gone so long."

She arrived home and removed the food and shoes from the trunk. She opened the bag with the shoes, removed the receipt, and tossed it into the trash can in the garage. She'd arrived just in time. Zach was just stirring as she entered the bedroom.

"What time is it? How long have I been asleep?"

"Hey, sleepyhead. You've been sleeping for, um, looks like about an hour and a half," Marcia responded as she looked at her watch. Her delay and looking at her watch was part of the act to show she wasn't quite sure and had to check. In reality, she knew exactly how long she'd been gone. "You need to get out of bed, sleepyhead," she said as she kissed him on the top of his head.

"Yeah, I guess I should get up. If I sleep too much longer, I'll be awake all night. Something smells great. Is that Chinese food I smell?"

"Yep, let's eat. I'm hungry."

While Zach went to the bathroom, Marcia dished up two plates, placed the bag with her new shoes on the barstool where Zach would see it, and awaited his arrival. As he got to the kitchen counter, he noticed the bag and paused to look into it long enough to notice the pair of running shoes.

"Oh, I see you finally got some new shoes," he said, putting the bag with the shoes on the floor. "I thought you got a pair a week or two ago. Didn't you?"

Marcia paused for a moment, trying to remember if Zach had actually seen her shoes and trying to determine the best response. Marcia was not a particularly good liar, so she needed a moment to think. "Oh, honey, I'm sorry. I forgot to move them off the seat," Marcia said, trying to change the subject and give her time to think of a good response.

"No problem," Zach responded quickly.

"You know these do look like the ones you showed me last week," he continued as he took another look in the bag.

"Yeah," she said slowly. "I had to change them for another pair. The inserts were defective, and they were just not right. This pair is much more comfortable."

"Good. Hopefully, this pair will be better for you."

Marcia just smiled at Zach. Because she was lying, the conversation was a bit awkward for her, and she wasn't sure of an appropriate response.

After a weird few seconds of silence, Zach finally said, "You know, you just reminded me that I need to look into purchasing a new pair also."

After quickly eating dinner, they retreated to the living room to watch a movie.

"So what movie did you rent?"

Marcia had been so caught up with reading Frank's records and thinking through her lie about buying new shoes, she'd completely forgotten about picking up a movie.

"Oh, yeah. Sorry, I checked the video machine at the store, and it didn't have anything worth seeing. Why don't we just rent something online?"

After a few minutes of searching the new movie selections, they decided on an action movie and spent the next two hours watching it. As soon as it was over, Marcia cleaned up and put away the leftover food, and then told Zach she had to check her e-mail.

"OK. If you don't mind, I just want to sit here and catch up to some light reading."

"No, not a problem," Marcia responded and gave Zach a hug and light peck on the lips. She quickly disappeared into their home office and started her search through medical journals for articles on resurrecting large dogs and pigs. Zach stayed in the family room and started reading a book he had started several months ago but had put away after becoming obsessed with Frank.

As Marcia searched, she came across an article that caught her interest. It was an article written by the assistant of a coroner from an Eastern bloc country. According to the article, a young boy had fallen into a lake in the Siberian woodlands and frozen to death before anyone could get to him. It took hours to rescue him and a second day to get his frozen body to a medical facility. Realizing the boy was an orphan, the coroner decided to experiment with the idea of trying to defrost the body slowly to see what would happen to the tissues. As he carefully and meticulously defrosted the body, he decided to inject warm spinal fluid he had drained from another body into the base of the boy's neck. At the same time, he injected the brain, heart, kidneys, liver, and lungs with a concoction of steroids, antibiotics, epinephrine, and the extract of a plant from the Limonium family he had found while on a medical expedition in Africa.

According to the rural African tribe, the plant, which grew wild in Africa, was the "life giver" and used only in the direst medical circumstances. The tribesmen shared that their tribal doctor was able to bring people back to life. When asked for proof, none was provided. Nonetheless, the doctor's research indicated the plant seemed to be one of the 125 or so species of the Limonium plant. Species of the plant, known by the name of statice, were often used by flower shops to accent bouquets, and somehow the flowers maintained their vibrant color months after they should be dead.

Numerous medical professionals had researched and studied this particular species, indigenous to Africa, but no one could pinpoint or agree upon what the plant did to the human body. There was a consensus that wherever this plant was found, the earth within thirty feet in any direction was the most fertile within miles. What was also unknown was whether the plant just happened to grow only in the fertile environment or if it contributed to the fertile environment.

This particular doctor's theory was that if he could get most vital organs functioning by taking advantage of the properties of the plant, he could treat the patient with the right mix of antibiotics and meds that would stimulate the remaining organs into functioning.

"Limonium plant and spinal fluid," Marcia said with a smile as she continued reading.

According to the article, the boy registered brain activity, and his heart worked for a full twenty-four hours before they both stopped for the last time. The boy was pronounced dead for a second time. When the World

Health Organization got wind of what happened, the coroner quickly cremated the body for fear of losing his license. His license as a medical physician had already been revoked for conducting inappropriate experiments on humans, so he had resigned to become a coroner. He was fearful that he would lose that license and would not be able to earn a living.

There was gleam in Marcia's eyes as she read the article. She knew she could do it. As a neuroscientist, she knew exactly the combination of meds she would need to stimulate the brain and how they would interact with the rest of the body. Now she had a good idea about what she needed to do to get the rest of the organs functioning again. The spinal fluid was easy; she had some at the office. As an extra measure, she also had a few cubic centimeters of brain fluid. As for the plant...

"Wait a minute."

"What's up?" Zach startled her as he walked into the office behind her. She immediately closed the web browser and jumped up to face him.

"Hi, honey. I thought you were reading."

"Yeah, but I got lonely and wondered what you were up to. You working?" Zach was trying to see over her shoulder to get a better view of the computer.

She stepped toward him to block his view and gave him a big kiss. "You're right. Let's quit reading and go open a bottle of wine and head to bed."

"Now, that sounds like a great plan to me," Zach responded.

"You go shut things down around the house and get a bottle of wine from the wine fridge, and I'll shut down in here. I'll be waiting for you wearing your favorite outfit," Marcia offered.

"I'm on my way. Don't be long," Zach said as he headed toward the door.

"Hey, hon, by the way, whatever happened to that plant sample you got from Africa?" Marcia asked casually.

Zach paused at the door, turned toward her, and thought for a second. "You mean that five-inch Limonium sprig that TJ gave me after his research trip to Africa?"

"Yeah, that five-inch sprig. Is it still alive?"

"Yeah, it seems to be. The purple flowers on it look just as bright as they did when TJ gave it to me last summer. It's on my credenza at the hospital. Why do you ask?"

That great news made Marcia excited. "What is it supposed to do?" she asked, intentionally ignoring his question.

"Well, according to TJ and his colleague Kenneth, the African tribe they got it from told them it causes unexplained growth or *rebirth* of just about anything."

Now Marcia was really interested. "What do you mean?"

"I don't know. I never figured it out, and I haven't been in touch with those guys for a while. I seem to remember them saying the tribe's doctor—they used the term 'witch doctor'—used it for healing those who were injured. They were even telling stories of the witch doctor using it to make zombies out of the dead. I'm not into witch doctors and zombies. I wasn't about to get into that discussion with them, so I didn't inquire any further."

"Didn't you ever test it?" Marcia asked, trying to quell her excitement.

"It's been a while, but I seem to remember it had the properties of many of the drugs we use for inflammation as well as growth hormones and a few other properties that escape my mind right now. I was too caught up with my work, and it didn't seem of much use to me, so I just put it in my office. Besides, my concoction of meds for my patients in my study is controversial enough; I dared not consider some sort of plant that doesn't have FDA approval." He gave her a look. "Why the sudden interest in my plant?"

Intentionally ignoring his question again, Marcia walked over to Zach and stopped within inches of his face. "Can I have it?" she asked in a sweet, melodic voice.

"When you ask like that, how can I say no? But why?"

Marcia batted her eyes at him. "Do you really want to continue this conversation, or do you want to go lock up the house and meet me upstairs with that bottle of wine?"

Zach didn't get an answer from Marcia, and he wanted to ask one more time, but he dared not bring it up again and lose out on getting more sex. They had been on a lovemaking drought for months. To do it twice in one day was an absolute treat that Zach was not going to pass up or mess up by saying the wrong thing.

While Zach turned off the lights, made sure the exterior doors were locked, and set the house alarm, Marcia had enough time to reopen the browser and delete her history before shutting down the computer. In a flash, she ran upstairs, changed into the outfit she knew he liked, and waited for him to show up. This second round of sex was just as passionate as the first.

They both hadn't realized just how much they had missed being together. They allowed themselves to get immersed in their jobs and had lost touch with the passion in their relationship for several months. At one point, it seemed obvious to friends and family that they were headed for a divorce. The way things were going today, divorce was the furthest thing from their minds as they dozed off to sleep.

The beeping from the alarm clock startled Zach as it woke him from a deep sleep. Marcia had already taken a shower and was in the process of putting on a little light makeup before getting dressed. As she heard the clock, she walked out of the bathroom to greet Zach.

"Hello, sleepyhead." She kissed him.

"Hey, babe, you're up early. Something special going on in the cryo department today?"

"No, just the usual stuff." She paused for a moment, trying to hold back the laughter as she followed by saying, "I freeze dead people." With that comment, they both started laughing. As movie buffs, they knew her comment was a play on a movie where the character said, "I see dead people."

"OK, that's a good one," Zach commented.

Zach got out of bed and headed to the bathroom. Marcia kissed him as he walked by. "I've got to go. Fresh coffee is on the counter. I'll stop by your office to get that plant, OK?"

"Yeah, but—"

She was already out the door before he could finish asking her why she wanted it.

In a few short seconds, she was on her way to work. On the way, she couldn't help but think about Frank and whether she was brave enough to conduct an unproven medical procedure on him. As she arrived at work and parked, she was still trying to make up her mind what to do. She was in such deep thought, she forgot to turn off the ignition. As she sat there, she started talking to herself to reinforce what she was planning to do.

"My experiments have worked on animals, but I was lacking spinal fluid and that plant in the equation. If this works, it will be a medical miracle. If this works, I could lose my license and go to jail. Ugh! What the hell, he's already dead. How much worse could this be?"

Suddenly, she was startled by a knock on the driver's side window.

"Hey, Doc, are you OK?"

"Huh…yes, yes, I'm fine."

"Sorry, ma'am. I didn't mean to startle you. I was just patrolling the parking lot and noticed your car running," replied the security officer.

She looked at him and jumped back. The officer looked exactly like Frank. Her face turned white as a sheet, and she looked away. Then she looked back at him with her eyes wide open.

"Are you all right?" he repeated as he opened her door, which she now had a death grip on that kept it from opening. On her second look, she realized it was William, one of the hospital security guards. As soon as she realized it, she let go of her death grip and assisted with opening the door.

"Doc, are you all right?"

"Yeah, yeah, I'm fine, William. I'm sorry, I guess I just didn't get enough sleep last night."

"No problem, Doc. Sorry about pulling on your door. It just seemed like something was wrong for a moment. Do you need me to call someone?"

"No, I'm good. I'm headed in to my office."

Marcia turned off the ignition, grabbed her purse off the passenger seat, closed the door, and hit the remote lock as she walked away. The security guard stood and watched her enter the building to make sure she was OK. As she entered the building, Marcia headed directly to Zach's office. It was locked. She went to the front desk and asked the security officer if he could let her in. Fortunately for her, it was William, who at this point was willing to do anything to make up for startling her earlier.

"Again, I'm sorry, Dr. Gage."

"No problem, William. I appreciate your opening up my husband's office for me."

"Normally, I wouldn't open the office, but because I know both you and Dr. Gage, I figure it should be all right."

"As I said, I just need to get a jar off his desk," Marcia replied.

"No problem, Dr. Gage, but I have to enter with you. OK?"

"Sure. No problem."

As they walked in, Marcia quickly spied the small bottle, about the size of a large jelly jar, sitting on the printer stand. She picked it up and looked at it. What it contained just looked like a five-inch twig with vibrant purple flowers. Zach had had the twig for the better part of the year, and the hospital staff had studied the properties of the plant as a potential source for helping with Zach's coma patients. Yet, as Marcia examined the plant, the flower buds still looked as purple and fresh as the day it had been removed from the ground.

"That's strange," Marcia observed.

Suddenly, the room echoed with a loud "Beep, beep, beep!"

"Dr. Gage, I have to lock the office back up. I'm getting a call from the office."

"No problem, William. Thanks for opening it up for me."

As they went their separate ways, Marcia realized she was feeling a little tired and thought a hot cup of coffee would get her back on track, so she diverted to the café. As she sipped the bland cup of java, she wished she'd stopped by her favorite coffee shop on the way in.

When she arrived at her old office, she noticed that some of Frank's records were not in the same place that she'd left them. She put down the jar and thought about the condition of his records for a moment before dismissing it as just another oddity of the day.

She quickly locked up and went to her current office. She started her morning with a quick meeting with her staff in preparation for the division meeting shortly afterward. By the time she got back to her office, half the morning was gone, and she was anxious to start working on Frank but knew she'd not be able to account for her whereabouts during the day.

Given how the morning had started, she decided to cut the day short and use some of her sick time. She met with her assistant, Angie, and told her she was headed home to take some sick hours. Her assistant seemed as if she were about to question her but decided to just end the conversation with "I hope you feel better."

Marcia stopped by Zach's office to let him know she was headed home, but he was out doing his rounds, so she stuck a handwritten note to his computer. Marcia went home, took a sedative, and went to sleep. She had to be prepared for phase two of her plan...to defrost Frank.

Chapter 11
DEFROSTING

After some five hours of solid sleep, Marcia finally woke up when Zach arrived home. He quietly entered the bedroom to check on her and saw her stirring as he walked in.

"Hey, babe, are you all right?"

"Yeah, I'm fine. Just needed some more rest."

"I brought you some seafood soup. You up for it?"

"Sure, let me run to the bathroom, and I'll be down."

"Oh no! I'll bring it up," Zach insisted.

"Aw, come on, Zach. I'm fine. I'll come downstairs," Marcia insisted. Marcia suddenly remembered that Zach normally treated her like a patient when she was sick, which was good but counterproductive to her plan to head back to the hospital later in the evening. As Zach paused to respond again, Marcia jumped out of the bed and slipped into the bathroom.

"Dish out my share, and I'll be right down," she instructed him from the bathroom.

Zach, realizing there was no convincing her, decided to leave it alone, so he served her food and waited for her downstairs. Within a few minutes, Marcia was downstairs sitting across from Zach, drinking her soup. As she drank, she wondered how she was going to tell him she needed to get back to the hospital…tonight. She was genuinely tired when she came home, but it was also part of her plan to have a reason to be in the hospital when no one from her team was around. In her head, she played out a couple of things to say and his reaction. Each scenario seemed to lead to the same conclusion: he was not going to simply let her walk out the door and go back to the hospital at night; especially because he thought she was sick. So it came down to either sneaking out—nope, that was too juvenile, plus he might wake up while she was gone—or just blurting out that she had work to do.

"Zach, this soup is wonderful. It really hit the spot. Thanks."

"I'm glad you like it," Zach replied.

"Honey, you know, I've missed several days of work over the last couple of weeks. I really need to catch up. Do you mind if I head back to work to take care of a few things?"

Zach thought about it for a moment. She saw his "patient/doctor" mode coming, so she headed it off.

"It will only be for an hour or so. I'm just behind on a few things."

"You know what? I'll drive you; I could use the quiet time to catch up on some paperwork. Maybe I'll check the system for Frank's autopsy report."

That was the last thing she needed to hear. Her eyes widened as she got up quickly to put her bowl in the sink.

"Zach, don't you think you should put that whole Frank thing behind you? I can't imagine the autopsy report will give you more than you already know. For the sake of your sanity and our relationship, why don't you just give the Frank thing a rest?"

Zach knew he really wanted to know what caused Frank's death, but right now he wasn't about to argue. He figured he would check on the report when he had time during the week and not give Marcia a reason to become upset.

"Yeah, I guess you're right."

That was music to her ears. To prevent another discussion about Frank and to reinforce Zach's willingness to not make a big deal about her request to leave the Frank situation alone, Marcia blurted out, "You know what, babe? Maybe we can just stay in and watch a movie on TV. I can catch up in the morning."

"You sure?" Zach inquired.

"Yeah, let's see what's on television.

After a couple of hours of mindlessly watching several comedy pro-grams on TV, Zach decided he would go for a run.

"Oh, so are you going for what, seven miles today? Or are you going to round it out to a cool ten miler?" Marcia asked.

"I'm thinking more like five to six. I need to get back here to check on you."

"Really? That's sweet, Zach, but I'm fine. I told you, I was just tired. Now I'm rested." She took his hand and placed it on her forehead. "Look, no temperature—see? You should go for at least eight or ten miles today. It will help you prep for the half marathon we're entering next month."

"No, you mean the half marathon you're entering. I'm just there for moral support," Zach replied.

"Either way. You can't help to pace me if you don't run the distance. By the way, did you realize we missed the Army ten-miler last month? I can't believe we're already into November."

Zach had heard enough. He knew further discussions would lead to being blamed for them missing the Army run last month. He needed to end the conversation before it became contentious.

"OK, ten miles it is," Zach finally replied. He got dressed and went outside to stretch. As soon as he stepped out the door, Marcia changed into a set of sweats and waited for him to leave. She watched him turn the corner and immediately jumped into her car, opened the garage door, and backed into the street. She set her watch to count down from one hour and thirty minutes. She knew he would take about an hour and forty-five minutes to run ten miles, so she gave herself a little extra time to get home and settle in before he returned.

Within a record six minutes, Marcia was at the hospital parking lot. She quickly swiped in the side door using her PIN and beelined to the overflow cryofridge in her old work center. She stopped in her old office to grab her coat and again noticed that the box with Frank's records was not in the same place where she had left it. She paused for a second to recollect where she thought she'd left it but quickly dismissed the thought, since she was on a very short timeline.

It took her close to an hour to remove Frank's body from storage and wrap him in the electromagnetic blanket to slowly defrost him. Based on her calculations, he would be 95 percent defrosted by the next evening, which would be enough to start phase two of the process.

After putting everything in place in the old surgical room, Marcia grabbed her keys, locked the room, and made a quick exit back to her car. She was home and in the garage in less than ten minutes and was just entering the kitchen when she saw Zach out the window stretching after his run. She was sweating and felt a little hot. Then she suddenly realized she was still wearing her lab coat. Zach was just coming through the door as she dumped her coat into the laundry bin.

"Hi, hon. How was your run?"

"Great. It was a perfect night to run. You should have joined me." Marcia just gave him a half smile. Zach walked toward the laundry room as he removed his shirt, which made Marcia nervous. She moved toward him to cut off his access to the laundry room, which also led through to the garage. She felt better when he stopped and reached into the fridge for a bottled water.

"You OK? You seem anxious or flustered."

"Why would I be flustered?" Marcia asked, trying to seem calm. She heard the crack in her voice and realized that pretending to be calm was not working.

"You know, it's the fact that my sexy husband just removed his shirt is what's got me flustered." She blurted out, a bit more calmly. Zach smiled at her as he strolled toward the laundry room. She knew he was headed to toss his shirt into the bin, so she quickly cut him off by stepping in front of the doorway, facing him, and slipping her arms around his neck to give him a big kiss.

"Wow, where did that come from?" Zach asked, a bit surprised.

"Oh, I don't know. Must be all that sweat. Let's go upstairs to take a nice warm bath. It will do good for your muscles after that run you just did."

"Sounds like a plan," Zach responded and moved to get to the laundry bin.

"I'll get that, Dr. Gage," she said as she took the shirt away from him. "Now, go on upstairs and get the tub filled up. I'll be right behind you."

As soon as Zach disappeared upstairs, Marcia reached into the laundry bin, removed her lab coat, deposited Zach's shirt, and then quietly scampered to her car and stuffed it under her driver's seat. In a flash, she was upstairs, removing her clothes as she approached the bathroom. She was still sweating after that close call, but Zach didn't notice as she stepped into the tub.

Chapter 12
NO TURNING BACK

The following morning, things seemed pretty normal in the Gage household. It was the usual routine of getting ready and deciding if they needed both vehicles at work, and, if not, who should drive. Marcia suggested they both drive since she still had to catch up to some work, given she'd been out of the office for a few days over the past week or so. Zach insisted that he had no problems staying late, but Marcia held out until he realized he wasn't getting anywhere and just conceded to traveling in separate cars.

The day was typical for both Marcia and Zach, with Marcia spending her day in a couple of meetings and working with her staff on several funded research projects. With Frank gone, Zach was spending more time with his few remaining research patients. He took the extra time to triple-check every patient's record because he wanted to make sure that whatever caused Frank to die was not going to happen to his other comatose patients. Besides, he was starting to feel a bit guilty about the extra attention he had given to Frank over the past seven months. During that time, he lost two of his six research patients. One family decided their loved one had been through enough and refused further treatments and another died due to complications mostly caused by his age. Somehow, he approached the loss of those patients as simply part of the nature of his work. Frank was special to him, but now he had to treat his other patients with extra care. For now, the remaining patients were all he had to continue his research.

Towards the end of the day, Dr. Emory paged Zach to his office. Upon arrival, Zach saw Dr. Emory leafing through some paperwork.

"Ah, Zach, come on in. Have a seat. I'll be right with you."

Dr. Emory put away the papers on his desk and reached into his briefcase and pulled out a thick folder with a number of glossy pamphlets and illustrations. On the front of the folder was the name of a medical conference. Zach recognized the name. He'd been trying to get to the five-day conference for years, but due to budget constraints, only the department chiefs were funded to attend. It was much too expensive for him to pay his own way, so for the past few years; he just had to get the post-conference literature from Dr. Emory.

Dr. Emory handed Zach the package and paused for him to look at it. "What do you think? Dr. Emory asked.

"Why are you handing me this?"

"Well, Zach, I need a favor. If I go to the conference this year, not only do I miss my daughter's birthday for the third year in a row, I'll also miss her cheerleading competition, which apparently, according to my wife, is a huge deal to her. She's going to be thirteen, and I think my Kathy will seriously serve me divorce papers if I'm not there to share these memories."

As Dr. Emory spoke, Zach was leafing through the paperwork. He already knew the agenda and most of the subjects to be presented and discussed. He'd been hoping for the opportunity to go. He kept his head buried in the pamphlets, allowing Dr. Emory to speak. On the inside, he was as giddy as a teenager on prom night, but he maintained a cool exterior as he listened.

"So, Zach, you know where I'm going with this. Can you attend? Everything is already paid for, and if I don't go, we forfeit seven thousand dollars out of the division's budget, and that will not go over very well with the hospital accountants. The hosting organization does not have problems with substituting attendees; they just don't accommodate no-shows or last-minute cancellations. We are way past getting the hospital's money back, given this conference starts tomorrow."

Zach nodded his head. "I think I can make it happen, but I need to speak with Marcia and make sure she's good with me taking off at the last minute."

"Of course, of course," Dr. Emory responded.

"What about my patients. Who is going to keep tabs on them?"

"I've already asked Dr. Johnson to cover for you. Granted, he's doesn't have the in-depth knowledge you do about your patients, but I will be here to run top cover and take care of anything that comes up." Dr. Emory handed Zach a red folder. "All the information you need regarding my accommodations and registration is in this folder. Fortunately, I'm not doing a presentation this year, so you don't have to do anything but attend the lectures and the panel discussions and write a brief report within a week after you return."

"Easy enough," Zach responded. "Wow, it's after four. I need to find Marcia and get home to pack and take off for the conference."

"Yes, you better get going. Thanks, Zach. You really got me off the hook with Kathy on this one."

"No problem. Glad I could help."

Marcia had just left Zach's office, where she left a note to remind him she would be working for another couple of hours. He was still in Dr. Emory's office, which made it easier for Marcia, since she knew he would still try to convince her to come home sooner.

Once she left him the note, she quickly headed back to her old work center. Zach came around the corner and missed Marcia by seconds as she took the stairs to the basement. Upon arriving at his office, he saw the note and figured he would rush home to shower and pack, then catch up to her on his way out. He knew she did not like to be disturbed at work, and, based on the conversations they'd recently had about how behind she was, he figured he would give her more time to catch up.

As Marcia approached her old office, the hallways seemed ominously dark, and she felt a weird chill run down her spine. She shook both her hands at the wrists.

"Nerves," she thought. She opened the door with her hands shaking slightly and went directly to the surgical room and got to work. Frank was thawing right on schedule. She checked his temperature and realized it was time for phase three.

First, she cut several thin slivers of the plant she got from Zach's office and ground it in a small blender.

From that pulp, she extracted just over a cubic centimeter of fluid. Marcia then started an intravenous drip with a concoction she used in her successful experiments on animals, which she calls LP5. She added heavy antibiotics and steroids to the mixture of drugs. She removed one vial of her spinal fluid, warmed it up slightly, and then looked at it as she prepared to inject the fluid into the base of Frank's neck. Finally, she topped off the syringe with half of the fluid she had extracted from the plant.

"OK, Frank, this is going to be tricky," she said out loud. She approached him on his left side then rolled his body toward hers, getting him on his side. With one hand supporting his head and keeping him in place, she used her right hand to inject the fluid into the base of his neck. The warm fluid slowly flowed into his vein, but, without circulation in his body, it stopped shortly after entering.

Frank's body temperature was now ninety degrees, so Marcia was able to connect him to the old dialysis machine that was stored in a nearby corner. After withdrawing a half pint of her own blood, she used it in the machine as a primer to get the circulation flow going. In a few minutes, Marcia had blood flowing thorough Frank's body. Within minutes, his color changed from a pale blue to a slightly discolored flesh tone. The old machine was working. Blood was being pumped through Frank's veins and organs.

Marcia's heart was pumping so hard it felt as if it were coming out of her chest. She looked for the epinephrine and loaded it into a syringe with a large needle. She added LP5, a mix of steroids, the rest of the fluid from the plant, and antibiotics. After taking a deep breath, she stabbed Frank directly in the heart. She searched for the approximate locations of the liver and kidneys and did the same until the syringe was empty.

She was being a bit more careless than normal, but, she figured, he was already dead; being off by a little here or there shouldn't matter to him or anyone else.

She set up the paddles for the defibrillator, turned on the machine, and waited for them to charge. Marcia rubbed them together as she waited for the whistle to stop, indicating it was fully charged. The jolt of 320 volts caused Frank's body to bounce so hard, it almost toppled off the bed.

Marcia paused for a moment to catch her breath. The excitement of the possibility of what was going to happen had her looking completely disheveled. Her hair was loose and frayed, and her eyes were wide with excitement. She was really starting to look like the proverbial mad scientist.

She took a couple of minutes to check and make sure all the equipment was still connected and functioning. Then she increased the defibrillator voltage to 340 volts. Within seconds, the whistle of the defibrillator indicated the equipment was almost ready for the next round.

The additional voltage caused Frank's body to rise in the air and twist into a huge arch before it slammed back with a thud on the bed.

The noise startled Marcia, and she looked around suspiciously and waited, as if anticipating someone rushing through the door. The static created from the defibrillator caused Marcia's hair to get wispy and stand on end. Her eyes were wide with excitement as she worked in an old room with old equipment and dim lights, she had the eerie, ominous look of a mad professor working in a lab. Her hair whipping around only added to what had unfolded into a maddening scene.

Marcia paused for a minute and just stared at Frank's body. She went from just trying a crazy idea to a sense of desperation. She suddenly felt she *had* to get his heart started. She knew circulating his blood through his organs could be done for a limited time, before the vessels started to fail from the abnormal pressure of a forced flow of blood. Time was ticking away.

She looked at the clock on the wall and back at Frank.

"What the hell—he's already dead. What damage can I do?"

In a flash, she ground half of the remaining plant into liquid and then mixed it with a large dose of her spinal fluid, her brain fluid, and several cubic centimeters of LP5. Without hesitating, she leaned Frank upward while holding his neck and shoulders with one hand and injected the large dose of her brew directly into his brain stem.

As Marcia raced against time to keep his organs from experiencing permanent damage now that they were defrosted and blood was being forced through them, she frantically searched in nearby cabinets and drawers for a surgical kit. The odds of one being there was next to...

"Bingo! There it is." In the bottom drawer was an old surgical kit, still sealed. The date for the sterilization had long since passed, but Marcia was on a wild ride, so for the moment, she didn't care. Besides, her patient was dead, frozen, and recently defrosted. What harm was an expired surgical kit going to do at this time?

Marcia quickly opened the kit and rested the towel on a tray she pulled up next to the bed. As she opened the towel, her eyes carefully and quickly searched for the instruments she needed: scalpels, forceps, multipurpose clamps, and several retractors. "Damn it, no forceps, and those clamps are not big enough."

Marcia became frantic for a few seconds and then remembered they sometimes kept one or two basic open-heart-surgery kits in her lab. They never performed surgeries in the lab, but they often dissected the animals and opened the chest cavities to retrieve their hearts and other organs to study their condition after defrosting them.

Marcia quickly exited the door and jogged down the hallway to her lab. After a few minutes of searching through the surgical kit cabinets, she found a kit labeled "Basic Open-Heart Surgical Kit."

"Perfect," she thought. Just to make sure it had the clamps and retractors she needed, she opened the kit and examined it.

"Yes." She beamed as she looked at the instruments.

Marcia rolled the instruments in the towel and returned to Frank's side as quickly as she had left.

She set the instruments on the tray directly on top of the other instruments. She was in too much of a hurry to care right now. Her only focus was to get to his heart before one of his major organs exploded from too much blood being forced into it from the dialysis machine.

She opened his hospital robe, exposing his bare chest. With the scalpel in hand, Marcia took a deep breath and made a deep and long incision just over his heart. She quickly grabbed the forceps and pried the chest cavity open so she would have an unobstructed view of his heart. In quick succession, she put the forceps and retractors in place, giving her clear but limited access to his heart.

Blood was starting to ooze out of the open area, causing her to feel an even greater urgency. The suction she was using worked, but like everything in that abandoned area of the hospital, it didn't work well as it was significantly underpowered.

She pulled the defibrillator she'd placed at the foot of the bed next to her. A quick search around the defibrillator produced a pair of long, narrow paddles.

"Thank you, Lord," she said as she changed out the larger chest paddles.

It was kind of weird using the Lord's name at a time when she was in the middle of playing God, but she was way too caught up in her plan to think about what she had just said.

Blood was now on her gloves, her lab coat, and virtually all the equipment. The room was slowly evolving into a real mad scientist's lab—and Marcia fit right in.

As she inserted the narrow paddles into the chest cavity around the heart, she flipped the switch to charge the machine. She took a deep breath and waited for the whistle to stop. As it stopped, 340 volts were sent directly through Frank's heart. The heart beat three times and then stopped.

She set it up again. This time she gave another dose of the concoction of drugs in the syringe, just prior to another shock. With the defibrillator now set at 360 volts, Marcia shocked the heart, causing a large splash of blood to cover her hands, arms, and even her face. She jolted back from the unexpected splatter so hard that she almost caused Frank to fall on the floor. As she paused to regain her senses, she was still blinded by the blood that had splattered on her face. Some even got in her mouth. She tasted the blood, but even the grossness of having his blood in her mouth was irrelevant.

What was important in that very moment was what she heard. She paused for a few seconds to listen more intently. At first she had to strain to hear, but within seconds, it was clear as day: she could faintly hear the beating of his heart.

She wiped her face with the back of her bloody sleeve just enough to open her eyes and confirm what she was hearing...yes, the signs of a rhythmic heartbeat were registering on the pulse monitor. Then suddenly his heart stopped.

"No, no, no!"

Marcia quickly recharged the defibrillator and with the determination of a doctor seemingly gone mad with ambition, she shocked Frank's heart with 380 volts. Again, blood spattered everywhere; this time it even got in her hair.

Again blinded by the blood, she listened intently as she wiped the blood from her face with her blood-soaked sleeve. Again, she heard what she was hoping for, a rhythmic heartbeat. As she cleared enough blood so she could see, she looked down into his chest cavity and could see the heart working as expected—no, better than expected. She dragged her way to the other side of the bed to check the electroencephalograph machine to see if it registered any brain activity.

She almost fell to her knees at what she saw. With her eyes open wide, she whispered, "Oh my God, I did it. I really did it. He lives again! He's freaking alive!"

She looked up at the old discolored ceiling tiles as tears rolled down her face and mixed with Frank's blood. She beamed from ear to ear and breathed deeply for a few minutes before the reality of the calamity in the room occurred to her.

"Holy crap, what a mess!"

Marcia spent another few minutes just looking at Frank's breathing and his heart pumping before she closed his chest using several large staples from the surgical kit. She spent the next hour cleaning up the room and equipment. She double-bagged the surgical kit and all materials, including her lab coat.

She quickly slipped out to her main office down the hall and deposited the bag in the trash can with the rest of the hazardous waste materials from her lab team. After a quick shower and change into the gym clothes she kept in her office, she looked at herself in the mirror and thought she looked normal. She realized as she was brushing her teeth that she might have consumed some of his blood. "Well, it's too late now," she thought. "At least, I know from his medical files he doesn't have any diseases."

After brushing her teeth and doing another quick check in the mirror to ensure she didn't have any blood residue on her face or in her hair, she quickly returned to check on Frank. She was literally shaking with excitement and just a hint of fear. She actually had brought him back to life. The problem was she was so caught up with wanting to bring him back that she never considered what the hell she would do if she succeeded.

"Oh my God, oh my God, oh my God—what am I going to do with him?" she thought.

Suddenly, her watch alarm went off, startling her. She had forgotten she had set it earlier to keep her from completely losing track of time. She looked at the time and realized it was approaching 8:00 p.m., so it was time to catch up to Zach.

"Damn it! I can't leave him here...not now."

After thinking about it for a moment, she decided her only option was to sedate him until she could figure something out. Sedating him was the last thing she wanted to do; she could cause his heart to stop if she sedated him too much.

Marcia knew she didn't have a choice. She could not take a chance of him waking in a dazed state and making noise. Although they were in a deserted part of the basement, she knew if security or one of the maintenance employees happened to be walking nearby, they would hear him. Marcia went back to her main office and removed a small plastic bag containing a mild sedative she and her team used on experimental animals. She returned to Frank and attached the bag to the existing IV tubes, ensuring she set it on a slow drip that would last throughout the night. Just as she finished, she heard the hallway door to the stairwell slam, which caused her to freeze in place. She listened intently for a few seconds and thought she heard her name being called. Marcia ran to the door and peeked out. She saw Zach heading aimlessly to her office down the hall and calling her name. She quietly closed the door, grabbed her cell phone from the desk where she'd left it when she first arrived in the room, and placed a call.

Zach was about to knock on the door when his phone rang.

"Hey, babe. I was just about to knock on your door. At least, I think it's your door. I just realized I've been down here only once in the past year or so, and I'm really not sure if I'm in the right place. I should come see you more. Anyway, could you open up for me?"

"I must have just missed you, hon. I'm in the cafeteria getting us coffee," Marcia whispered into the phone.

"OK, I'll meet you up there," Zach whispered back. "By the way, why are we whispering?"

Marcia paused for a couple of seconds trying to come up with a quick response. She knew she was whispering to avoid the outside chance of him hearing her from the hallway.

"Lady with a sleeping baby nearby."

"OK, got you. See you in a few." She waited by the door until she heard the slam of the stairwell door. She quickly exited the old lab, ensuring the door was properly locked, and then darted for the exterior exit door. She was in such a rush that she forgot to wait the two seconds needed to disarm the door after she swiped her card.

As she ran through the door, it set off the alarm, causing Zach to double back to see what was going on. Within a few seconds, the alarm system got the signal indicating there was a swipe before the door was opened and shut itself off. By the time Zach got to the hallway, he wasn't sure which door alarm had gone off. He walked up to the exterior exit just to check it. That's just when a member of the hospital security team showed up to see what was going on.

"Can I help you, Doc?" the security guard asked.

"No, I heard the door alarm and decided to check on it. I thought I was down here by myself, so it startled me."

"Our sensors indicate this door had been opened. Did you see anyone?" the young security guard inquired.

"No. I just came down to catch up to my wife after getting a call from her in the cafeteria. I was headed upstairs when I heard the alarm."

The security guard swiped his card and opened the door to look out, after which he closed it and checked it was locked.

He turned and said, "Must have been a glitch in the system. I'll put it in my shift report so the morning shift can check into it further."

"Sounds good," Zach responded and headed back to the door leading to the stairwell. He held the door for the security guard then ascended the stairs. As he got to the first floor, he headed left down the hallway toward the cafeteria and arrived at the entrance just in time to see Marcia's smiling face and two cups of coffee.

Zach said, "Hey, thanks, babe," and greeted her with a kiss.

"Wow, I haven't seen you all day," Marcia responded.

"Why are you in sweats? That's not what you wore to work...right? Did you just come back from a run? I thought you were working."

"I *was* working. I...I dumped some chemicals on my clothes, so I had to shower and change. This is all I had in my office," Marcia responded rather clumsily. She was trying to keep a pleasant smile, but the last few hours had her on such an adrenaline rush that her smile looked fake and awkward. Zach noticed, but he had his own issue of having to break the news about leaving for the next five days; he dared not open the conversation with something that might get Marcia upset. He just smiled back, equally as clumsy.

Marcia wanted to change the subject quickly. She was looking for anything to talk about except her. She looked Zach over and noticed he wasn't wearing the clothes she had seen him in earlier.

"So why do you look so casual? This isn't what you wore to work this morning."

"Oh, yeah, about that. Let's sit down for a minute." Zach reached for her hand and led her toward a nearby table and sat down. "Babe, you know how for the last three years, I've been trying to get to the medical conference in Maryland."

"Yes, and?" Marcia inquired.

"Well, I'm finally getting a chance to go."

"That's wonderful," Marcia said excitedly.

"The problem is, it's tomorrow, and I have to leave tonight to check in and get situated for the meetings in the morning," Zach said quickly as he looked at Marcia with pleading eyes as he waited for her response.

This was the best news Marcia had heard all day—exactly the break she needed so she could focus on Frank. She had to contain her excitement at the great news. Marcia bit her lip and shifted in her chair in an effort to keep her composure. "So...so how long will you be gone?"

"I'll be gone for five days starting tomorrow. Well, technically, I leave tonight, but all in all, it's five days. It's a quick five days, though." Zach followed that up with half a smile.

He knew their relationship had been strained over the last several months, and they were just starting to turn the corner on rekindling the spark. This was definitely not the best time to leave, but it was the only reasonable chance he had to get to the conference. All he needed was for Marcia to be understanding. Zach had already made up his mind that he was going. He needed this conference to see if he could get some contacts to further support his research. But he wanted to know he went with Marcia's blessings.

"Zach, I know this is important to you. Don't worry about me. I'll be fine. This will give me a chance to really catch up and even work on the paperwork for my next grant. Can't start too early, you know."

It was exactly what he wanted to hear.

"Marcia, thanks for understanding. I figured you would support me, but I didn't anticipate you would accept the news so easily. Thanks. You're the best." Zach reached over and gave Marcia a soft kiss on the lips. As they kissed, Marcia's eyes were wide open, staring off toward the nearby wall, where she caught a glimpse of the clock and realized it was after 8:30 p.m.

She suddenly pulled back. "Hey, what time do you have to be there?"

"The conference check-in is at seven, but I need to get there tonight to avoid the maddening DC traffic in the morning."

"I don't want to push you out the door, but you better get going. You have at least a two-hour drive, and it's already after eight thirty."

Zach looked at his watch. "Yeah, you're right. I need to get on the road."

"Do you need to go home and pack or get your stuff, or were you so sure I'd buy into this that you are leaving from here?" Marcia asked while she put her left fist on her hip and waited for a response.

Zach looked back with a sheepish smile. "I'd banked on getting your support, so I'm already packed. I was prepared to bribe you with a romantic weekend getaway at our cottage, but I guess I don't have to do that now," Zach said, smiling.

"You turd!" Marcia replied, giving him a light tap on his shoulder. "I still want my romantic weekend getaway. I freaking deserve it, especially letting you off the hook that easily."

"OK, deal. Figure out when, and I'll take you."

"That's better." Marcia smiled. "I'm headed home anyway, so I'll walk you to your car." Marcia stood up.

At the car, they kissed and hugged, and Marcia stood in the parking lot watching Zach drive away as she waved. When he was no longer visible, she turned toward the hospital entrance. The smile on her face was replaced with an intense scowl that made her look a bit psychotic. Marcia went to the basement and directly back to Frank.

Chapter 13
CONNECTING

As Marcia headed back into the hospital, she replayed the situation over and over in her head. "I have five days. I have five days. Five days to do what, exactly?" she thought. On the way down, she stopped by Zach's office to borrow his tape recorder. The spare key he gave her just before leaving came in handy as his office was locked.

By the time she got back to Frank, she'd determined she had to get him out of the lab within those five days. Marcia was basically making up the plans along the way. She never thought about the fact that her experiment would actually work or what to do when it did. Marcia looked at the wall clock across the room; it was almost 9:00 p.m.

She put on a new lab coat, grabbed her stethoscope, and started a toe-to-head examination of Frank. As she conducted her exam, she recorded every observation.

"This is the case of an unknown male, approximately thirty years old. His name is Frank." She paused for a second, realizing that no last name had been assigned to him. It was something that no one had thought about. He was simply a John Doe they'd chosen to nickname Frank because of his resemblance to the famous 1960s singer and performer Frank Sinatra.

"His name," she continued, "is Frank Stein," using her maiden name. Marcia smiled a devilish smile as she said the name again in her head. "He died about a week ago of complications resulting from a fatal fall, which put him in an unrecoverable coma for some seven months. He was cryogenically frozen and was revived using a slow thaw while administering doses of LP5 experimental drugs used to regenerate cells after being cryogenically frozen; plus epinephrine, antibiotics, extract from the Limonium plant, and spinal and brain fluid taken from Dr. Marcia Gage. This mixture of drugs was injected directly into his lower brain stem, his heart, kidneys and liver."

Marcia looked him over as she spoke. "His color and complexion are slightly chalky white. I anticipate more color over time as the skin is exposed to sunlight. Toes seem to each move without restriction, and ankle joints show mobility. Slight bruising on the left ankle. His knees indicate he has mobility there as well. His fingers, hands, and arms all flex as normal. His incision...what the...oh my God!"

Marcia could not believe what she saw when she pulled back his robe. She was startled, so she stepped backward. After a few seconds, when she collected herself, she leaned in closer to get a better look at the place on his chest where she had made the incisions to place the paddles to jump-start his heart.

"His...his incision in his chest cavity...it's..." She paused as she stammered, trying to get the words out. She looked even closer and reached forward with her right hand to touch the wound.

"It's almost healed. It looks like a wound that's weeks old," she whispered in disbelief into the recorder. "But I made this incision only a few hours ago."

She stopped the recording and the exam for a couple of minutes and just stood there staring at his naked body. She noticed that the discoloration of his feet that she had documented only a few minutes ago had cleared up to match the rest of his chalky color.

She continued recording. "His face has regained some coloring closer to flesh tone."

She opened his mouth and had to lean back as the stench of his breath emanated toward her. It was almost toxic and caused her to heave as if she were going to gag. Tears welled up in her eyes from the pungent smell. She swore she literally saw a green smoky film leave his mouth. "Whoa, we've got to do something about that smell. Breath is horrible; teeth seem fine; gums are a healthy, deep-pink color."

She then dimmed the lights and used her flashlight to look into his eyes. As she opened his left eye, she watched his bloodshot eye, with tiny capillaries bulging, clear up to a smooth off-white color. His pupils reduced to a tiny pinpoint within a second of her shining the light into his eye. "His pupils respond to light...more rapidly than I'd expect. This response, I'd expect to see from a nocturnal animal that's not accustomed to light...hmm."

She checked his right eye and observed the same results. To ensure she could have a better tactile sense of what she was feeling, she removed her gloves and then rubbed—no, more like caressed—his face, as she checked his skin and facial bones. She finished off the exam running her hands through his hair. She had to catch herself; she was no longer conducting an exam, but rather she was admiring him and enjoying the sensation of touching his hair.

She got herself back on track by searching for a syringe in a nearby drawer and using it to remove a small sample of blood, which she placed under a microscope to observe. After a few seconds of looking at the blood, she continued to record her findings.

"Nothing abnormal found in blood based on visual observation using an electron microscope. In my professional opinion, patient Frank appears to be in good health. His body is recovering at an alarming rate. It's too soon to determine which combination of drugs contributed to that phenomenon. This concludes the examination, time now..." Her eyes searched for the wall clock. "Time now, ten forty-five p.m."

Marcia was starting to feel the effects of working long days. She just wanted to get to sleep. She put the recorder into her pocket and covered Frank with a sheet. She paused for a few seconds to admire his body, and then finished covering him. She checked to ensure there was enough sedative to keep him comfortable and to stop him from waking up in the middle of the night. Then she headed to her old office, where she removed the digital tape and placed it into the top desk drawer.

She sat at the desk, thinking about what she just had observed. Then, after a few minutes, she got up and checked his dialysis machine and did a second check on the sedatives before she caught herself, realizing she had done that just a few minutes ago. She figured with Zach out of town, she could easily come back in the morning and check on him. After she was satisfied that everything was in order, she headed home and called Zach on the way.

"Hey, babe," Zach answered. "I'm just pulling into the hotel parking lot right now. Where are you?"

"Almost home."

"Wow, you spent a long time at the job after I left. I thought you were headed home."

Marcia realized Zach had just caught her in a lie, since she'd told him she was headed home when she told him good-bye in the parking lot earlier.

"Um, ah, yeah, I went back to the office to check on one thing, and the next thing you know, a couple of hours had slipped by. By the way, I borrowed your recorder. I wanted to document my findings on one of my test cases."

"That's fine. Please just put it back in my drawer in time for my morning rounds when I get back."

"No problem. It will be there."

"Thanks. Well, I'm at the hotel now. I'll call you back after I check in."

"No, that's fine. I'm really tired. I just got home, and I'm going straight to bed. Call me when you get a chance during the day tomorrow. That way, you can let me know how things are going."

"OK, sounds good. Get some rest. Love you."

"Love you, too."

As Marcia entered the kitchen, it dawned on her that she hadn't eaten anything since a quick bite at lunch. She was hungry, but now sleep was more important. She quickly headed upstairs and went to bed.

That night she had the first of the nightmares that would haunt her for the rest of her life.

Chapter 14
GETTING INTO HER HEAD

Marcia drifted off to sleep within minutes. As she dozed off, she couldn't help but think about Frank and the events of the last couple of days. By 2:00 a.m., she had sunk into REM sleep and was dreaming about the time when she was running in the marathon and suddenly made a misstep that caused her to twist her ankle and jar the vertebrae. The excruciating pain she felt in her dream rapidly increased her pulse from a well-rested sixty beats per minute to a racing ninety beats per minute. Suddenly she was sitting up straight up in bed, her eyes wide open, looking across the room at the clock on the wall.

Except the scene she saw was not her room. It was in the lab where Frank was resting. She looked around in a daze in such a way that it didn't seem as if she were controlling her own head. It felt as if someone was making the movements for her. She could faintly hear the muffled sounds of what sounded like hospital equipment running in the background.

Suddenly, she felt a pain in her chest, right over her heart. She clutched at it, looking up at the ceiling tiles like the ones under which Frank was resting. She sat in bed trying to deal with the excruciating pain. Shortly afterwards, she felt a sense of euphoria, which caused her pulse rate to slow. As it slowed, her vision of the room got blurry and pinpointed with a haze around it, as if she were looking through a tube. The soft sounds became distant in a slow, methodical way as she drifted back to sleep. Her limp body flopped on her pillow, and she grazed her forehead on the edge of the nightstand.

Four hours later, the sound of the alarm clock jolted Marcia from sleep. She quickly sat up in bed. She looked around, a bit startled at the time, and thought how good it was that last night's episode was just a bad dream. As she started to get out of bed, she noticed her pajamas were completely soaked with sweat.

"Wow, what a weird dream," she thought. "I must have had a rough night...I sweated like a pig. Now I need another shower."

Marcia quickly hopped out of bed, grabbing underwear, a simple pair of pants, and a shirt, and headed to the bathroom. As she stood in front of the mirror brushing her teeth, she noticed a bruise on the top of her forehead. Her eyes widened as she leaned forward to get a closer look at the wound. It was a fresh mark about half an inch long where it was obvious she had simply scraped the skin. She backtracked to the bedroom and checked the nightstand carefully.

It didn't take more than a few seconds to find the small sliver of skin dangling from the corner of the nightstand. She ran her hands through her hair while looking at her ceiling; it was an eighteen-foot recessed ceiling with crown molding.

"What's going on? This is just too weird."

Marcia went back into the bathroom, took a shower, got dressed, and headed to work.

On her way to work, her cell phone rang. It was Zach.

"Hi, honey. How are things so far?"

"So far, so good. I just checked into the conference, and I'm having some of their buffet breakfast before the sessions get started. What a spread for breakfast. No wonder this conference is so expensive."

Marcia didn't respond to his comment.

"Hey, you OK?" he asked.

"Yeah, yeah, I'm fine," Marcia responded after a few seconds of silence. "I had a bad dream last night that kind of freaked me out."

"Want to talk about it?" Zach asked sympathetically.

"No. Not really. It's probably just because I was sleeping without you." Marcia did her best to sound cheerier. "You know how I am when you are not home. I miss you!"

"I miss you, too. Do you need me to come home?" Zach cringed as he asked the question. He was really doing it to show his concern, and he was hoping for a confirmed "no." In less than two seconds he got what he hoped for, but it did surprise him a little.

"No! I mean, no," Marcia responded, realizing how quickly and loudly she'd spoken. "You've wanted to attend the conference for years. Now you are finally there. Enjoy it, and get as much as you can out of it. I'm fine. It's just a stupid dream. Besides, maybe you can land a new sponsor to fund your research. Call me later tonight before I go to bed."

"OK, good. Yeah, I hope I can land a sponsor. I'll call you tonight. Looks like most people are going into the main conference room to check in. I better get going. Love you."

"Love you, too."

By the time they finished the conversation, Marcia was turning into the hospital parking lot. As she parked, she realized she'd driven past her favorite coffee shop.

"Ugh, I hate starting the day with bad cafeteria coffee," she mumbled to herself.

It was a few minutes after seven, and her staff was not due to arrive for another twenty minutes, so she took the time to slip down the hallway to check on Frank before heading to her office. She was not prepared for what she saw. Frank and his sheets were soaking wet, as if he'd sweated the whole night. As she did a quick once-over of Frank to make sure he was all right, she noticed a fresh cut on the top left corner of his head. It was in the same position as hers.

"Oh my God, what happened?" Marcia said softly as she put her hand over her nose and mouth, trying to filter the foul odor that was emanating from his body.

She checked her watch and realized she had only fifteen minutes—best-case scenario—to fix this problem and get back to her office before her staff arrived. She slipped out of the door, went to her current lab area, and grabbed a couple of gowns. She looked around for bed sheets but was unable to locate any.

"These will just have to do for now," she said to herself as she scurried down the hall. She was in such a hurry, she didn't see Angie, her twenty-nine-year-old assistant, standing in the dark corner down the hallway, breaking company rules about employees using cell phones in the hospital as she texted her boyfriend, apologizing for the fight they'd had the previous night.

At first Angie was surprised, but then she got curious as to what Marcia was doing. She watched her enter the old office area and close the door silently. It was some ten minutes before she saw her again, this time with a handful of damp sheets.

Angie and Marcia didn't see eye to eye most of the time, and it would be great if she could get some dirt on Marcia that she could use to give her some leverage to get her way more often. After seeing Marcia go into the old work center several days ago, Angie had snooped around, but didn't see anything but some files on a patient name Frank. Now that she saw Marcia going back and forth, she was starting to figure she needed to check the work center again. Angie stayed flat against the wall in the little closet space and watched Marcia go by and enter their lab. She gave her a minute and then went in so Marcia would not know what she had seen.

Most days, Angie and Marcia spoke to each other only when they needed to. They were both professional, but Angie saw Marcia as a showy doctor who had had her success given to her, and Marcia saw Angie as a spoiled brat who really didn't want to work. Their perceptions of each other shaped their conversations so that they were always filled with underlying tension. Truth be told, each was a bit jealous of the other. Angie would die to be like Marcia, and Marcia wished she could be more free spirited, especially with men, as Angie seemed to be, despite having a live-in boyfriend.

Today, Angie was going to figure out what was going on down the hallway and that meant initiating a conversation.

"Good morning, Dr. Gage." Angie smiled as she approached Marcia's office.

Marcia was a bit startled. "Oh, hi, Angie. I didn't hear you come in. How are you doing?"

"I'm fine. What about you? Everything OK?" Angie was peering at her as she asked the question.

"All is well, Angie. Listen, I need to go over these lab reports. Could you do me a favor and check the status on the specimens from last week?"

"Last week?" Angie queried.

"Yes, last week," Marcia replied, sounding a bit irritated. She really didn't even remember what specimens, if any, had come in last week. She just wanted to end the conversation.

Angie picked up on the irritation in her voice, and although she instinctively wanted to push Marcia's buttons to figure out what was going on down the hall, she decided not to pursue things for the moment and played along.

"Sure, sure, I'll go check on last week's specimens."

Angie walked away even more curious about what she had seen, and she vowed to herself that she was going to get to the bottom of it. By God, she was not going to allow Marcia to work on some secret project and take all the credit instead of sharing it with the team.

Angie kept an eye on Marcia from a distance for any telltale sign of anything suspicious, but the day, and Marcia, seemed like business as usual. Marcia appeared a bit more wired than she typically was, but she'd overheard her mention to someone that Zach was out of town, and she didn't sleep well when Zach was not in the house. Angie thought that was surprising because only a few short weeks ago, the rumor throughout the hospital had been that the Gages were on the verge of a divorce. Everyone was saying how they had grown apart because of her husband's obsession for a patient.

At the end of the day, Angie and Marcia were the only ones from the team left working. Marcia was trying to finish paperwork she was using as an excuse to stay late as she waited for everyone to leave. She knew that at the first opportunity she had after the team left, she would be down the hallway checking on Frank. Angie, on the other hand, was simply stalling to see if Marcia would eventually head back to the old office. An hour and a half after the last staff member had left; Marcia looked at her watch and realized it was past 6:30 p.m. She desperately wanted to get back to Frank, but with Angie there, she dared not risk her discovering what was going on. Marcia was tired anyway, and getting home at a decent hour was starting to look like her best option. At 6:40 p.m., Marcia shut off her computer, removed and hung up her white lab coat, and bade good-night to Angie.

"Angie, I'm tired. I'm headed home to eat, shower, call Zach, and go to sleep."

"OK, good night. I'll finish a few things before locking up. I'm not far behind you," Angie replied.

Marcia nodded, acknowledging her comment, and then waved as she closed the door. Now that it appeared that Angie was going to be tied up for a few minutes, Marcia decided to take the chance of doing a quick check on Frank. She was too tired to leave without checking on him, since going directly home now would mean a return trip late at night.

As she closed the door, she quickly and quietly jogged down the hall toward the old office. After a hurried look around in both directions to ensure no one was nearby, she swiped her card and entered her code to open the door.

She spent a hasty ten minutes disconnecting the dialysis machine, checking his vital signs, and conducting a head-to-toe visual inspection. Two things were of note: his wound was healed, and he had an erection. She dimmed the lights and quickly slipped back into the hallway, first checking to make sure she wouldn't run into Angie.

In a flash, she jogged up the stairs and was outside the hospital, headed toward her car. She was tired but was feeling pretty good about what she had accomplished in resurrecting Frank.

Marcia wasn't even out of the parking lot before Angie stepped out of the shadows of the hallway and headed toward the room in which Frank was located.

Chapter 15
THE CONNECTION

Angie went to the door, swiped her badge, and entered her PIN. It worked like a charm. Hospital security personnel were good at patrolling the hospital and keeping the parking lot safe, but removing one's access to the facility after employment terminated or an employee moved from one location to another was a systemic problem in the IT department. As the chief of the cryogenics department, Marcia appropriately had access to the old office area, but no one else should.

Angie opened the door slowly, peering from behind it, not knowing what she would find on the other side, this time. As she entered, her nose picked up a musky smell, and she could hear the faint sounds of a heart monitor coming from what used to be known as the "clean room," where bodies and human parts were processed for freezing. She tiptoed across the room and peered into the clean room. She could just make out the shadow of a person on a bed placed conspicuously in the middle of the room.

Stealthily as a cat, she snuck up to the bed from behind the head of the bed and peered over. With a gasp, she jerked back, placing her hands over her mouth to stifle a scream. As she stood there, she second-guessed what she saw.

"It couldn't be," she thought.

Realizing that the person hadn't moved, she slowly and carefully shifted into a position where she could get a better look. She immediately identified him as the John Doe everyone called Frank. She saw his records the last couple of times she visited, but this was her first time seeing him in person. She remembered seeing his face on the TV when they were searching for his relatives and friends. She squinted her eyes as she tilted her head to the side.

"I thought you were dead," she said to herself. "I could have sworn you died." She kept playing it over and over in her head.

She continued to stare at his face for a few seconds, almost mesmerized by his good looks. "Wow, you're cute," she said out loud. "Now, let's see what the rest of you looks like."

She carefully moved to the side of the bed and took a moment to look him over. First, she pulled back his cover. Then she untied his gown and pulled it off, exposing his body.

"Very nice, very nice," she said slowly as she noticed his toned physique. She also noticed his skin was slightly opaque and rubbed her hands across his chest, touching what appeared to be a healing wound in the middle of his chest.

Frank's left hand reached up and grabbed her wrist with such quickness and force that she never saw it coming. Angie let out a muffled scream and tried to yank her arm away, but he had a grip on her like a vise. With her left hand, she grabbed his and pried each finger away, creating enough of a gap for her to pull away. As she turned to run, she noticed his arm didn't move; it remained in the same bent position as if frozen in place.

She was freaking out about what just happened, but she felt compelled to stay. Her right wrist was throbbing, and red and blue welts were starting to form.

Angie rubbed her wrist while standing some twenty feet away, trying to figure out what she should do next. One part of her wanted to run down the hallway screaming; the other part wanted to know why a person who was supposed to be dead was alive and breathing. After Angie calmed down, she came to the stark realization of why Frank was lying alive on the bed.

"Son of a...she freaking did it! She brought him back to life." The words echoed in her head, and what this meant finally sank in.

"Oh my God, she experimented on a human being." Angie stood there just staring at Frank, realizing that he represented proof positive that bringing someone back from the dead—and maybe after being frozen— was indeed possible. As Angie stared at Frank, she deduced that Dr. Gage must have frozen him, since his slightly opaque skin was consistent with what she observed in the animals they experimented on.

A million questions floated in her head, but for now, she just needed to get a drink—a strong one. Knowing Frank had been brought back to life compelled her to stay and stare at him for a while. Angie slowly walked over to Frank's bed. As she walked, she paid particular attention to his arm, which was still bent upward with his hand open. She covered him with his hospital gown and blankets as quickly as she could. The whole time, she was leaning backward, poised to run at the first sign of any movement. She did it so quickly she forgot to retie the strings of the robe as she'd found them.

She was still rubbing her wrist as she left. Angie was shaken by the incident and what she had discovered, but she wasn't sure what to do about it. She went straight home, took a hot shower, and then downed several drinks, trying to calm her nerves. She wished her live-in boyfriend was there, but they had had a fight the night before, and she'd kicked him out. He was spending the night at a friend's apartment.

She did not sleep much that night.

In the morning, Angie woke up suddenly after having a disturbing dream of zombies chasing her. As she sat at her tiny dining table drinking freshly brewed coffee from her preprogrammed coffeemaker, she started to think about what she had seen last night.

At first she felt a little creepy, but as she really started to think about it, she realized that Marcia would take credit for all the work. After two years of working with Marcia on dozens of failed experiments, she was damned if she would let Marcia take all the accolades for bringing some- one back from being frozen. "By God," Angie thought, "I deserve some kudos, too." If it weren't for her efforts of conducting research and studies and carefully documenting each case side by side with Marcia, the doctor would never have gained the knowledge she needed to bring Frank back from the dead.

The question in Angie's mind was how to go about it. Angie's perspective changed from feeling apprehensive about Frank being alive to figuring out just how much fame and money she would share if the world knew about this success story.

Marcia, in the meantime, was just getting off the phone with Zach. He was due back in three days, and she knew she had to get Frank out of the hospital before he returned. She realized that the only way to get him out of there was to get him conscious and checked into another facility.

"I need time to work on him," she said out loud to herself. She reached for the phone and called Angie.

"Hi, Angie. It's Dr. Gage."

Angie pulled the phone back and looked at it in disbelief. "Oh, hi...hi, Dr. Gage. Is everything all right?"

"Yes, I just need to take care of a few things today, so I'm taking a personal day, but I wanted to make sure you were up to speed on the list of tasks we need to complete today."

"Yes, I'm good. I know where you left off yesterday. I'm good. I'll keep the team going."

"Oh, thank you."

As Marcia spoke, Angie was itching to ask her about Frank. "Dr. Gage..."

"Yes, Angie?" After a long uncomfortable pause, Marcia asked again, "Angie, are you still there?"

"I'm still here. That's fine. Will you be in tomorrow?"

"I plan to be. I just need today to take care of some personal errands. Figured with Zach out of town, this would be a good time to take care of them. Thanks for covering."

"No problem, Dr. Gage."

Marcia got off the phone and then called her boss to let him know she planned on taking a personal day and that arrangements had been made to cover the department workload.

As soon as she got off the phone, she got on the Internet to search for a facility that offered assisted care with rehabilitative services. Several hours and numerous phone calls later, she narrowed her options down to a couple of places within ten minutes of the house, but only one had an immediate opening.

Armed with that information, Marcia headed to work but parked her car in the visitor's lot in an attempt to blend in and keep anyone from realizing she was there. She quietly made her way to the basement's side door, swiped her access card, entered her PIN, and then jogged to the old office.

Marcia knew she had only a couple of days to get Frank prepared to transition to a rehabilitation center, so she went to work immediately upon arrival. As she approached Frank, she noticed that his sheet wasn't pulled up all the way as she had left it. Upon closer observation, she noticed his robe didn't look right. As she checked it, she noted the robe's drawstrings were untied.

She was sure she had tied the robe on him. She dismissed the situation and started a complete head-to-toe examination, using Zach's recorder to mark her notes.

"Mark on left forehead is completely healed after approximately twenty-four hours; however, the facial scar he had when he died still remains. Skin color continues to become more flesh tone. At this rate, I anticipate his skin to appear completely normal in the next twenty-four hours. Surgical incision on chest is nothing but a red scar at this point. This is remarkable. It's unknown at this time which combination of medications caused this rapid healing. It would appear that marks or scars that occurred prior to resuscitating the patient stayed in place; new cuts, however, heal within days or hours. Amazing!"

Marcia continued with the examination down his torso to his groin area. She couldn't help but pause for a second to admire him. It was only a few seconds, and then she refocused on checking his legs and feet, again noting that everything seemed normal. She then rolled him over and conducted a physical check, starting with the base of his skull, checking his back, and working her way to his feet.

"This is absolutely incredible. A complete physical shows signs of a completely normal and healthy thirty-year-old man." She carefully returned him to his back and completed her examination, checking his eyes, ears, nose, and mouth.

She took a sample of his blood to check his cell condition but then decided it was time to try to wake him up. Zach would be home in a couple of days, so it was important for her to get Frank out of the hospital and into a rehabilitation center. With his progress so far, Marcia felt certain that she could pull it off before Zach returned. Marcia went over to the medication cabinet, which she had been slowly stocking from the supplies in her current work center.

"OK, let's see, a little epinephrine, some steroids, and ammonia should about do the trick." While she waited a few minutes for the medications to get into his bloodstream, she removed the oxygen tubes from this nose so she could wave the ammonia under his nose. A few waves later, Frank gave a loud "Aaaaaahhh," followed by heavy coughing, filled the room and could be heard down the hallway. They were fortunate that none of her staff was in the hallway passing by.

Frank jolted a few times, then he starting breathing erratically. Marcia immediately put the oxygen tubes back in place, which caused him to take several deep breaths before he calmed down. After a minute or so, he seemed to be breathing normally again.

Maria also calmed down a little. She touched her chest above her heart and could feel her heart beating so hard, she was sure, this time, it *was* coming out of her chest. She was so excited; she could hardly stay still. She decided that given his progress, she no longer needed the dialysis machine and went to disconnect it, when she realized she hadn't reconnected it from the other night.

"Good grief, his blood has been circulating on its own," she said out loud. She also wondered how he would do without the forced oxygen tubes in his nostrils. She slowly removed both tubes and monitored him for a few minutes. Nothing changed on the system monitoring his heart, pulse, and respiration.

"So far so good, but I've got to take a look at his blood cell count," Marcia dictated as she conducted the quick look to ensure she had accurate records of the entire procedure.

She placed a small sample of his blood on a specimen glass and looked at it under the high-powered electron microscope she'd borrowed from her other work center. "Oh my God! No freaking wonder! His blood cells are huge. I didn't see that before. They are at least twice normal size. And there are so many. Wow!" She caught herself and got back to the recorder to speak into it.

"It appears the patient's biological system has taken on an incredible ability to rapidly heal itself since his resurrection." She thought about what she just said and erased the last recording and repeated it using a different choice of words. "It appears the patient's biological system has taken on an incredible ability to rapidly heal itself. I removed all life-sustaining equipment, and all vital signs remain normal. I will continue to monitor for about an hour and will make another attempt to bring him out of sedation."

As Marcia waited, she continued with yet another thorough examination. She checked his ears, his eyes, and every inch of his body, pausing once again to admire his midsection. Then she looked down to his feet. She looked for any abnormalities and even bedsores and found nothing, absolutely nothing out of the norm. In fact, except for the scar he had received in the accident, Frank was the picture of perfect health—maybe too perfect.

It was time to start the process of bringing him out of his slumber. An hour ago, she had stopped his mild sedative and added some adrenaline and three cubic centimeters of the concoction Zach put together to revive patients out of a coma. She was apprehensive about using a medication she didn't fully understand, but she figured with his remarkable recovery, and his body's ability to heal itself, it was a risk she could take. After all, what was the worst that could happen? He'd die.

After injecting Frank with the mixture, Marcia sat beside him and looked for any sign of him coming around. Within ten minutes, she noticed his fingers twitching. From there, the twitching seemed to work its way up his arms and through the rest of his body, all the way to his feet. As the twitching stopped, she heard him give a low moan. She immediately went and stood by his head and started a process of rubbing his temples while talking to him.

"Come on, Frank. I know you can hear me. Come back to us. Come back."

His moan got a little louder. The louder he got, the more she spoke words of encouragement to bring him out of the sedated state. After a couple of minutes, she sat him upward at the waist and started to gently shake him while whispering, "Wake up, wake up, wake up." Suddenly, without warning, his eyes opened.

Chapter 16
MAN OR MONSTER?

Marcia gasped. She looked into his eyes, and for the first time, they looked back. Her grip on his shoulders loosened for a second. Then, realizing his body would simply flop back onto the bed, she regained a firm grip. Marcia's mind was racing. She was flooded with elation, and she couldn't help but stare back into his mesmerizing eyes.

Marcia and Frank stared at each other for a full ten seconds before Marcia finally blinked. It was as if each were trying to outstare the other. Frank also blinked as if imitating Marcia. It was getting a little odd for Marcia, so she finally broke the stare by looking away, which made Frank move his head and cock it slightly to the right as if questioning what she was doing or where she was directing her attention. It was a robotic, awkward move. Marcia figured it was as a result of fracturing his neck.

In her observations, he healed quickly, but there seemed to be residual effects from anything that had happened before she brought him back to life. His head bobbled a bit like those bobblehead toys, but in a few seconds, he steadied his head as if a bolt of energy had suddenly surged into his neck muscles.

Marcia took note of what just happened, which caused her to again lighten her grip so she could back away from him. She could feel him slipping straight back to the bed and braced herself for his 180 pounds to slam into the mattress and pillows, when in slow motion, his back, shoulders, and head stopped just short of touching the mattress and the pillows, and he popped back up in the same position where she'd been holding him a few seconds earlier. It was as if his muscles, which by all accounts should have atrophied and required weeks and weeks of physical therapy, simply relearned proper movement in a matter of seconds.

After a few minutes of observing him, she noticed the only time he blinked was when she did when she was staring at him. So she tried to turn his face to directly face hers and noticed his shoulders turned with this neck, indicating some stiffness, again probably due to his fractured neck. As he looked into her eyes, she started blinking hers every three to four seconds. He watched her and then followed suit. After a minute or so, he started blinking on a normal cycle, about every four to five seconds.

After another half hour of evaluating Frank, Marcia realized she need-ed to figure out what to do with him now that he was conscious and appar-ently might not need a rehab center.

"Should I put him in an apartment, an extended-stay hotel, or still put him in a rehab center, where he will at least be watched twenty-four seven," she wondered. Her mind raced for a minute as she tried to figure out what to do with him.

Marcia decided to see if she could get Frank admitted to the rehabilita-tion center near her home. It was the only place that made sense to her at the moment.

She placed her hands on his shoulders and slowly laid Frank down and went to her old office to make the call. A few minutes into the call, she heard a crash and immediately looked to see if Frank was OK. She got to him in time to see him floundering like a turtle on his back, trying to get up.

As she went over to assist him, he literally jumped to his feet. He was a little unsteady, so she helped him back onto the bed and laid him down. She looked him in his eyes and said, "Stay here."

Marcia was starting to feel less comfortable about the rehab center, not knowing what questions they would ask and whether they would discover there was no record of him anywhere. He had no ID, no social security number, nothing to register him as you would any other law-abiding citi-zen. Marcia knew she needed him to spend another night in the hospital.

She retrieved a mild sedative and injected Frank with just enough to make him sleepy. After a few moments, the medication settled in, and Frank seemed to be resting comfortably. It was now 5:00 p.m., and Marcia realized she had been there all day and had not eaten. With Frank back in place, she cleaned up the mess he'd made, checked the hallway for anyone, and swiftly jogged down the hall toward the side door.

Unfortunately, she ran into Angie.

This time, Angie was intentionally hiding in the corner waiting for Marcia to leave. She'd heard the crash just as she was leaving the work center and stuck around to see what was going on.

"So hello, Dr. Gage. What are you doing here?" Angie inquired.

Marcia was startled and a bit taken back because it seemed like Angie was waiting for her to exit the old lab. "Oh…oh…OK…hi, Angie. I was just here to pick up a couple of things from the office. Where did you come from?"

"The office," Angie replied with a smart look on her face, as if to say, "I know you are lying to me."

"Funny. I didn't see you in there."

"Yes, funny, isn't it, Dr. Gage?" she said after an uncomfortable pause. "So what are you doing in our old work center, Dr. Gage?"

"Excuse me?" Marcia stated, annoyed that Angie was questioning her. Her attitude only added fuel to the fire.

"I said…"

"I heard you the first time. Listen, you don't ever question me! Do you understand?" As Marcia spoke, her vision blurred for a few seconds. It was as if she were suddenly in a poorly lit room. She stared at Angie but did not see her.

She rubbed her eyes with the back of her right hand, hoping that would clear her vision. Her pulse raced. She was not only irritated by Angie's behavior, but now she was having trouble seeing properly. As she peered forward, she saw Angie and the hallway for a few seconds, and then she saw the walls of a poorly lit room with what looked like an analog clock on the wall. As she forced her eyes to focus on what looked like a familiar clock, she heard Angie's voice.

"Oh my God, Dr. Gage. Can you hear me? Are you all right? Are you all right?"

Marcia squeezed her eyes and pinched the middle of her nose with her thumb and index finger. When she opened her eyes, she realized she was sitting on the floor of the hallway with Angie rubbing her right shoulder and asking if she was all right. It took Marcia a few extra seconds to focus. Angie was within inches of her face, apparently trying to get a good look into Marcia's eyes to determine her alertness.

"Ah, yes, Angie. I'm all right." She finally got the words out. "I'll be all right."

"What happened?" Angie asked.

"I don't know. One minute I was talking to you and the next..." Marcia trailed off and looked down the hallway toward where Frank was being kept. "And the next thing I knew; you were asking me if I'm all right."

"Let me get you some water," Angie volunteered. She helped Marcia to her feet, and they walked toward their current work center, pausing just long enough for Angie to swipe her card and enter her code to gain access. Within a few minutes of the incident, Marcia was sitting at one of the counters in the lab space, drinking a cup of water.

"Angie. Have you been into our old office space recently?"

"Yes," she replied rather smartly as she rubbed her right wrist from the recent incident with Frank. Angie was poised to suddenly start asking a lot of questions but decided to hold her tongue and just let Marcia speak.

"Well, then, you know what—I mean, who—is in there...right?"

"Yes, I do."

"I'm guessing you want to know why he's in there."

Angie just looked at Marcia. The look said it all.

"Of course you do. Well, here's the thing: he never really died. I took possession of him from the orderly and resuscitated him within minutes. Then I decided to keep him down here to study him further."

Angie wasn't buying it, but she didn't want to be confrontational and get Dr. Gage worked up again. So she was tactful in what she asked.

"So why didn't you just take him back upstairs after you resuscitated him?"

"Well, with the media and all, I didn't want to bring too much attention to our lab down here. People kind of know what we do here, but if they fully understood the extent of our work—like including the fact that we are basically a morgue with dozens of frozen bodies and even frozen heads in storage—the community would take a different view about us being here.

"If I took him back upstairs, it would generate a lot of unwanted and uncontrolled media attention. I couldn't risk the negative impact it would have on our work."

It sounded like a good answer, but the media wasn't really keeping up with Frank. He was just another John Doe as far as they were concerned.

Angie knew she was lying. She stood there for a moment, deciding her next move. "Does anyone else know about him?"

Marcia shook her head. "No, just the two of us. I would like to keep it that way for now. Can you do that, Angie?"

Angie ignored Marcia's question. "Can I see him?" Angie asked, trying to contain her enthusiasm.

Marcia thought about it for a few seconds. "I really don't think that's a good idea."

"OK, no problem. We'll see what our boss and the media think about your little project."

Realizing she was being blackmailed into taking Angie to see Frank pissed her off. She knew she had no recourse, but she still tried to get out of it. "How do I know you won't tell everyone after I take you in there?"

"You don't, but I can guarantee you I *will* tell if you don't take me to see him."

Angie had the upper hand, which made Marcia fume.

"OK, I'll take you to see him, but promise me you'll keep this between us. This work is too important to be sabotaged at this point."

"No, Dr. Gage, it's too important to hide from the world. Remember, your ability to do whatever it took to bring Frank back after freezing him was the result of the blood and sweat of your entire team, and now you cut us out of the glory."

"How did you know I froze him?"

"Actually, I saw some telltale signs from the condition of his skin, but I wasn't sure until now," Angie responded with a smug smile.

Marcia rolled her eyes as she realized she had basically admitted to freezing him simply by her response to Angie. Marcia felt desperate and figured she really didn't have a choice. "Just promise me you won't tell anyone," she pleaded.

"Let me see him, and tell me how you did it, and I promise I won't say anything. Oh, and when you finally release the information about him, I get to share the credit for being your right-hand person for years, which led you to this success."

Marcia bit her lip and didn't say a word. She simply led Angie back to the room and swiped them in. They entered the room, and on their way to where Frank was located, Marcia tried once more.

"Angie, promise me you won't talk," Marcia said, speaking more loudly now that they were out of the hallway. She was ready to agree to Angie's terms, but she needed reassurance that Angie was not going to go to the hospital staff or the media. Marcia was visibly getting more upset, but Angie wasn't paying attention to her. She was singularly focused on Frank as she approached him slowly.

"Angie!"

No response. Angie was still focused on Frank.

She stood over Frank, admiring his face and realizing that he was not connected to any machines. She walked around the other side of the bed, which allowed her a view of Marcia and Frank at the same time. Angie caressed Frank's face and pulled back the covers slowly. "How do you think you can continue to hide him? You must let everyone know. He is a gift to the world."

She slipped her phone out of her pocket and raised it just high enough to take a picture of Frank.

As she spoke, Marcia continued to get more anxious and angry. As she saw Angie's phone, she knew she needed to stop her from taking a picture and broadcasting it to the world.

"Angie, don't!" Marcia screamed.

She knew she'd broken a number of laws, flaunted medical ethics and hospital policies, and trashed at least a dozen other rules. Letting word out about Frank right now would ruin her personally and professionally. She had been so focused on treating Frank that she had not taken the time to think through how she would break the news of her accomplishment or handle any of the backlash it would cause once the world knew what she had done.

One thing she knew for sure; she was not ready for this conversation or for Angie to have proof that he was still alive. Marcia was starting to sweat and get angry again.

Suddenly, she felt faint, just as she had in the hallway. She was starting to fade to the floor. She blinked her eyes a couple of times, and when she opened them, she was looking at Angie from a different perspective. She was seeing Angie's lower jaw from under her chin. It took her a couple of seconds to realize she was seeing Angie from Frank's vantage point.

Angie continued talking as she got the camera on her phone ready to take another picture. "This is an absolute breakthrough..." Angie started to say.

In the split second it took Marcia to blink, Frank's left hand swiftly reached up and wrapped tightly around Angie's neck.

Angie stopped midsentence as she felt his powerful hand crush her esophagus. Her eyes bulged as she dropped the phone and grabbed his hand with both of hers, trying to get him to let go. Marcia's vision was back, and shocked, she stood there frozen for a few seconds as she watched in horror. Seconds later, she cracked a half smile as she watched Angie's body go limp as she slumped on Frank's outstretched arm.

Marcia's problem was solved. Angie was no longer going to able to broadcast what she knew about Frank.

One side of her wondered, what the hell had just happened? Her other side felt Angie got what she deserved. "How dare she challenge, blackmail, and threaten me," she rationalized.

Oddly enough, she didn't seem to wonder or care about how or why Frank had reacted that way. The whole situation was so surreal that Marcia felt she was having an out-of-body experience.

Marcia slowly walked over to Frank and peeled his fingers from Angie's neck. As if in a trance, Marcia instinctively dragged her limp body toward the old cryogenics preparation center. Within fifteen minutes, Angie's body was sealed into one of the cylinders and put into storage in the old refrigeration unit. It was a quick job, and she skipped a number of steps, but she thought, "Who cares? It's not as if I'm going to bring her back."

When she was finished, she went back to Frank and did a quick visual check. He was peacefully resting, so she patted his shoulder, dimmed the lights, and left via the side basement door. She never noticed Angie's phone, which was wedged between the mattress and the bed rail.

Chapter 17
WHAT TO DO WITH HIM?

By the time Marcia got home, she was physically, mentally, and emotionally drained. She took a quick call from Zach, and then she filled the tub and soaked for thirty minutes before going to bed.

The fact that Frank had strangled and killed Angie didn't bother her. It was as if she were suddenly living a surreal life. She dozed off to sleep without giving Angie a second thought.

The next morning, Marcia was awakened by the telephone.

"Hello," Marcia said tiredly into the phone.

"Hi, Dr. Gage. I'm sorry to bother you so early in the morning. I'm Angie's boyfriend. Angie didn't come home after work yesterday, and I was wondering if you'd seen her."

Marcia was in a daze after being awakened at 5:30 a.m. She needed a moment to think. "I'm sorry, but who is this again?"

"This is Tim, Angie's boyfriend. We met about three months ago in the hospital cafeteria. Again, I'm sorry to call so early, but I held out as long as I could after calling the hospital, all our friends, and even a couple of family members. You are the only person I know from her workplace. We had a fight the other day, but this is her place, so she always comes home." Tim sounded frantic, and he was speaking so fast Marcia couldn't keep up. "Have you seen her, Dr. Gage?"

"Um, no, Tim. I haven't seen her. I wasn't at work yesterday. Angie was covering for me while I took care of a few things at home."

"Oh, ah, OK. Thanks, Dr. Gage. I'm sorry to bother you. Please let me know if you hear from her. My number is..."

As he told her the number, Marcia responded with "OK, got it. I'll call if I hear from her."

The response was so quick that Tim was pretty sure she hadn't written his number down. She was out of sorts when he woke her up, and he was pretty sure she just got him off the phone and didn't write down his number.

After hanging up, Tim took a deep breath and thought about calling the police. The only problem was he didn't have anything to go on. He had no reason to suspect foul play; all he would be able to tell them was that this behavior wasn't like Angie.

He was starting to get more worried by the minute, and he decided to go by the hospital to see if her car was still there. Within thirty minutes, he was able to confirm that Angie's car was in the parking lot. He texted her a couple of times from the parking lot, praying she would respond. Her car was covered with morning dew, indicating it had been there all night.

"Where the hell would she go without her car?" Tim thought.

After a few minutes, he went inside to speak with security. He had never been to her office, but he knew she worked in the basement, and she was required to swipe her access card to gain entrance. The security officer was empathetic but refused to give him any information regarding the last time she'd entered her office since Tim was unable to produce any proof that she was his wife, as he'd told him.

When he got back to his car, he took a deep breath and dialed 911. Tim reported Angie as a missing person, but although he was directed to an investigator who took the information, he was instructed to call back if she remained missing for over forty-eight hours. At this point, given she'd been gone fewer than twenty-four hours; the police had no intention of taking any action. Tim was frustrated and helpless.

As he sat there trying to figure out what to do next, he saw Marcia arrive and park near the side basement door. He thought it strange that she didn't park in the area reserved for staff members.

Angie often complained that Dr. Gage had her own parking space in the staff parking lot, and although she was her deputy, she was not high enough in the organizational structure to get into the reserved staff parking area, much less get her own personal space. That meant Angie often spent several frustrating minutes driving around the parking lot, looking for a place to park.

"So why in the world would Dr. Gage park near the side basement entrance?" Tim thought.

As Marcia exited her vehicle, she made a concerted effort to scan the parking lot to see who was around and, at one point, dodged behind a van to avoid being seen by a security guard cruising by in the hospital golf cart. Tim's tinted windows kept her from seeing him, but he still sat motionless to ensure his movement or silhouette wouldn't cause her to notice he was in his vehicle. He sensed something wasn't right, and the way she was behaving just confirmed his suspicion.

Tim stayed in his car to watch what would happen next. He figured if she went into the side door, odds were that she planned to take something out that door that she didn't want anyone to see.

Twenty minutes later, his suspicions were confirmed. Marcia came out the door, trying to her best to prop up a tall, gangly gentleman wearing ill-fitting slacks and a shirt.

"What the hell? Who is that? And why is she sneaking him out the back door?" Tim asked himself out loud.

First Angie went missing, and now Dr. Gage seemed to be smuggling some guy out of the hospital. As he watched Dr. Gage help the man toward the passenger side of the car, he decided to confront her. He figured he had nothing to lose, given the situation, so he scurried over to Dr. Gage.

He got to her just as she assisted Frank into the passenger seat. She was reaching to help him with his seat belt when Tim's cell phone rang. Tim was now directly behind Marcia, and the sound startled her. She suddenly stood, severely banging her head on the doorframe, and the blow knocked her to the ground.

Tim was also startled but quickly looked at the name on the phone before answering. "Angie, where are you? Where have you been?" Tim yelled into the phone, only to hear himself in stereo. It sounded like his voice was coming from the car. "Angie?" he said again into the phone only to hear himself again a fraction of a second later. "What are you doing with Angie's phone?" he yelled at Frank. "Where is Angie? What have you done with her?"

As he spoke, he approached the door, stepping over Marcia, who was still dazed from the bump on her head.

A few minutes later, she regained full consciousness, only to find she was lying in Frank's hospital bed with Frank standing over her and wiping her forehead with a wet rag. As she sat up, she looked around and saw Tim's limp and motionless body curled into a fetal position on the floor.

"How did we get here?" she asked Frank. He responded by simply pointing to her badge, indicating he used it.

"But it uses a PIN. How do you know my PIN?

Frank shrugged his shoulders. "I know it," he mouthed. No sound came out, but she knew what he had said.

Marcia got up from the bed and walked over to Tim. As she rolled him over, her hand touched his chest, and she felt something odd. She raised his shirt to find a handprint across his chest that had caused his chest cavity to cave inward. It was apparent that Frank had shoved Tim so hard that he had collapsed his chest plate and ribs into his heart. The entire area was badly discolored, indicating internal bleeding.

"Oh my God, Frank. You did this?"

Frank tried to respond, but only a throaty grunt came out. He held his throat and tried two or three more times with the same result. Frustrated, he stopped trying and nodded his head while he mouthed, "Yes."

Marcia then noticed one of the storage vats was sitting in the middle of the room.

"What's that doing there?" she asked him while walking toward the vat. As she walked over to the lab area, she realized Frank had completed all the prep work to cryogenically freeze Tim. Everything was in place, awaiting Tim's body.

Marcia walked around dazed. How was Frank able to do this by himself? It took months of supervised training to accomplish what Frank had just done. As Marcia stood there perplexed, Frank was busy removing Tim's clothes. He then placed him into the vat and closed the lid.

Marcia watched him handle the equipment step by step from a memory he shouldn't have. Several steps he took were exactly the way Marcia did the procedures.

"How in the hell is he doing this?" she wondered. "He never saw me do those procedures. This doesn't make sense. Does he have my knowledge from my spinal and brain fluid?" she asked herself quietly.

She watched Frank change into Tim's clothes because they were a better fit for him. Frank had completed a complicated set of procedures that normally took an expert close to an hour to finish in almost half the time. As he completed the final step, Frank pushed Tim's body into the storage freezer next to Angie's.

Marcia was at a loss for words. She had watched a man who was dead just a few days ago complete a set of complicated procedures without a checklist better than any expert she had ever seen.

After he closed the freezer door, Frank stood in front of Marcia. He had Zach's clothes—the ones he had been wearing only moments earlier—bundled and tucked under his arm. He motioned that he was ready to go.

Without saying a word, she took Frank's hand and led him into the hallway to the basement exit. Once there, she asked him to show her how he got in. Frank gently took her badge, swiped it, and then entered her four-digit PIN so quickly, it was like he'd created the pin himself.

"How? How do you know this, and how do you know how to freeze someone?"

Just then they heard the upstairs door slam and footsteps coming down the stairs. They quickly slipped out the exit door, jumped into Marcia's car, and then drove away.

With Frank now walking, he obviously no longer needed physical therapy. Marcia had figured she would have at least a few weeks while Frank was in a facility to figure out a long-term plan. Now she was stuck having to execute a plan immediately.

She didn't know where to go, but she knew she couldn't just randomly drive around and risk being seen with him.

"I was going to take you to a place where they would assist you with physical therapy. I'd assumed your muscles had atrophied, given you have been in a bed for so long in a…"

Marcia realized she was about to tell him he'd been in a coma and later died and was frozen for several weeks and resurrected only a few days ago. She quickly changed tactic. "You were bedridden for several months after having a concussion in an automobile accident."

As she spoke, she realized she really had nowhere to put him. She thought about hotels, but that would generate too many questions. He no longer needed physical therapy, and that facility would also generate even more questions. What now? After thirty minutes of driving around downtown DC, they finally ended up in the parking lot where they had started.

Frank, puzzled, looked at Marcia. "Frank, I have nowhere to take you. Do you have a house, an apartment?"

Frank shrugged his shoulders, indicating he didn't know.

"Let's go back inside."

In a few minutes, they were back where they started, in the basement work center that had been his home since his death. At this point, Frank looked pathetically sad, but he understood that Marcia didn't have a choice. As he sat on one of the barstools at a worktable, his stomach suddenly growled loudly. Marcia got the cue.

"Yes, I imagine you are hungry. I'll go get you something from the cafeteria. I'll be right back."

Within ten minutes, Marcia was back with so much food that even the cashier commented, "So where is the party, Doc?" Marcia only smiled at the cashier and hurried back to the office. When she got back, she saw Frank rummaging through Angie's purse.

"Let's put this away where it can't be found," Marcia said as she closed the purse and put it in her old office. "I didn't know what you wanted, so I got you a little of everything. Pick what you want for now, and we'll store the rest in the refrigerator."

Frank didn't need any coaxing to eat. He had been surviving on the nutrients provided through an IV since he was brought back from the dead. He had no idea when he had last eaten a meal, but at that moment, it didn't matter. The only thing that mattered was that he had a smorgasbord in front of him, and he was ready to eat. The part about portioning out some for now and storing the rest for later was completely lost on him.

As Marcia left him for a few minutes to log on to her computer and do some online searching about the plant she'd used on Frank, he went to work and devoured everything in a matter of minutes. He literally ripped through the chicken and breakfast sandwiches using his hands.

Marcia was too caught up in her Internet research to notice what Frank was doing to the food.

"Wow, he's really freaking alive," she thought as she sipped her coffee and scrolled through page after page on her computer screen. She knew she needed a place to put him, but she also needed to know what she was dealing with. She wondered if Frank was likely to be violent toward her—or just toward people who threatened her.

Marcia's mind raced from one subject to another as she clicked her mouse. "On one hand, he seems like an absolute genius, knowing how to freeze Tim and figuring out my badge code. Yet he seems both childlike and psychotic in some of his behavior. How could he just kill two people in the last two days with no conscience about his actions?"

As the words echoed in Marcia's head, she suddenly realized her own reactions to Angie's and Tim's deaths seemed abnormal. She had basically no emotions about what Frank had done to them. It was as if her capacity for remorse was gone...completely gone.

"Why don't I feel anything?" Marcia queried herself. Just as that thought entered her mind, she found a set of articles. One was about the observations of a professor who studied an Indian tribe in Guatemala, where this plant was found in abundance. As she scanned the study, she found that the professor documented that the chief's wife had died during childbirth and been brought back using the plant.

According to his observations, she seemed to be the most intellectually advanced tribe member, but she was also more violent and ruthless than anyone else. Although traditionally women were not allowed to participate in disciplining the tribesmen for infractions against the community, she not only participated, but she was so violent that she killed two young and vibrant tribesmen for what the group considered minor infractions. The article described her as showing symptoms of bipolar disorder and lacking a conscience.

"Oh my..."

Just then she saw Frank run by her office toward the bathroom. She jumped up to follow him to see what was going on. He barely made it before he started throwing up. For the next several minutes, he heaved and upchucked all the food he had just eaten. He sounded horrible, and all Marcia could do was rub the back of his head as he made loud heaving noises into the toilet.

As he lost this meal, Marcia realized she hadn't been thinking when she left him with so much food. She expected him to drink the soup and eat some of the bread she bought. She had no expectation that he would dig into what was planned for tomorrow's breakfast and lunch.

Frank had not eaten in months, so his stomach was unable to process so much food, especially all at one time. Marcia felt terrible, knowing that as a doctor, she couldn't do any more than rub the back of his head.

As she looked down at Frank, she finally took stock of the situation she'd created. Here was a man she had brought back from the dead. She knew nothing about him: his background, his personality, nothing. Now that he was here, he seemed to be exhibiting strange capabilities, like healing a hundred times faster than normal. He seemed to be twice as strong as a normal human, yet he was also childlike.

To top it off, he seemed to do things without any conscience, just like the native in Guatemala. Come to think of it, she had observed the death of her assistant and boyfriend, and it hadn't bothered her in the least.

"What's happening to us?"

Frank finally got to a point of dry heaves, so she knew he was done. She assisted him to stand up, and he promptly rinsed out his mouth using the mouthwash on the sink.

He looked flushed.

"You going to be OK?"

Frank nodded, still looking a bit out of sorts.

"You need to take a shower. It would make you feel better."

Again, Frank nodded.

Marcia helped him remove his shirt and unbuckled his pants, which immediately fell to the ground, exposing the fact that he was not wearing any underwear. A bit embarrassed at noticing he was very aroused, Marcia turned to walk away. With his right hand, Frank gently grabbed her hand and motioned her toward the shower which is normally used for washing off anyone or anything they planned to freeze. He turned on the shower with his left hand and walked into the flowing water, which literally glistened on his skin.

For the first time, Marcia really took note of what a complete physically attractive package he was. She had realized he was handsome, but she never quite looked at him in such a sensual and sexy way. Right now, he was wet, aroused, and waiting for her in the shower. Although Zach had been gone for only a few days, Marcia's loins were aching for some manly attention.

After some twenty seconds of trying to reconcile what the rational side of her brain was telling her to do with the craving she was having for him, she finally stepped into the shower wearing all her clothes. Frank peeled her clothes off her body, tearing her shirt in half in the process. Without her uttering a word, Frank methodically worked her body like a violin in the hands of a master musician. He did everything she enjoyed; it was as if he had cracked the code to her body's sexual needs.

When it was over, Marcia had experienced the best sex she'd ever had in her life. Afterward, she helped Frank get situated in bed and asked him to not leave the room while she was gone. He nodded to show he understood and would comply with her request.

Marcia had nothing to change into, so she put on her wet clothes after the shower. Luckily, she found an old scrub shirt in her desk drawer and pulled it over her torn shirt. Still in damp clothes, she fled the hospital to her car in the parking lot. She arrived home ten minutes later. As she closed the garage door, she removed her clothes and dumped them into the hamper and scooted upstairs naked, heading for her bathroom to take another shower.

As Marcia showered, she went through mixed emotions. She felt she was floating and then felt guilty for having cheated on Zach, and then went back to floating on cloud nine since this was absolutely the best sex she'd *ever* had. She was still floating as she got out of the shower and started changing. Suddenly, the phone rang. It startled her.

"Hi, Zach. How are you?"

"Hello? Is this my wife? Hello?" the voice on the other end responded.

"Yes, Zachary, it's me."

"You OK?"

"Yeah, I'm OK. I think I'm just a bit tired."

"I'm sorry. I tried to reach you earlier, and I was starting to get worried. You really sound down. Is everything OK?"

"Yes, everything is fine. I was just working a few extra hours since you were not here. It gave me a chance to catch up."

"Well, make sure you don't overdo it. I'll be home tomorrow night, and I would like to spend some quality time with you."

"OK, sure, sounds good," Marcia replied, doing her best to sound jovial. "Do you want to go out for dinner when you come home, or do you want me to make your favorite dish?"

"Shrimp dinner? Wow, that sounds great. I can't wait until tomorrow to see you. I can't believe I've been gone for a week. It feels more like several weeks when I'm away from you."

Zach paused, waiting for a response from Marcia that would indicate she'd missed him too, but nothing came. He decided to get a response in another way.

"It's been great coming here, but I really missed you."

"I missed you too. Listen, Zach, I'm really tired. It's been a long week, and I was just getting ready for bed and—"

"I understand. I'll get to see you tomorrow anyway."

"Thanks for understanding. By the way, what time will you be home?"

"I should be finished here in the afternoon around three, and with traffic, I think I should be home by six."

"Sounds good. I will see you then."

Zach paused to hear her say, "Love you." But after an uncomfortable silence, he took the phone from his ear and stared at the receiver with a puzzled look on his face. Finally, he said it, and Marcia responded with "Love you too."

"Wow, that was a bit strange," he thought. She had seemed distant and even a bit indifferent during the whole conversation.

"You would have thought that after being apart, she would be truly missing me, not just saying the words," he thought out loud.

Anyway, he knew he had better get started on the summary report from the conference that he had promised to his boss. After that, he got distracted with the agenda for the next day. He needed to decide which seminars he was going to attend so he could use his time most efficiently.

After about an hour, he decided to go to bed. He lay awake for at least an hour, thinking about the rather chilly conversation he had had with his wife earlier.

"I wonder what's wrong," he asked himself as he dozed off to sleep."

In the meantime, Marcia was also having a difficult time getting to sleep. Her thoughts were on Frank. She wasn't feeling guilty or ashamed for having cheated on Zach. Instead, she was trying to figure out what she was going to do with him long term. In the short term, she was trying to figure out how she could get him to make her feel the way she'd felt earlier.

"Damn!"

Chapter 18
CONFLICT OF INTEREST

With a loud, orgasmic yell, Marcia suddenly jumped up in bed to find she was drenched in sweat and that she'd just climaxed. She was having a dream about being with Frank, and it got so passionate that it woke her up. During the encounter, she felt she clearly saw the room in which Frank had been sleeping. It all seemed so real it was difficult to determine if it had happened. As she removed the covers, she discovered a bruise on her right thigh and suddenly recalled bumping her leg in the heat of passion in her dream.

"It was a dream, wasn't it?" she questioned herself as she ran her left hand through her hair. "How did I get this bruise?" she queried as she ran her hand over it trying to remember some other time in the last twenty-four hours that it might have happened.

Nothing came to mind, but every time she closed her eyes for more than a few seconds, visions of her being with Frank came to mind. It was as if she kept reliving an encounter that had never taken place. It was during that encounter that she bumped her leg.

"Am I losing my mind, or am I hallucinating?" she said out loud.

After pondering for a few seconds, she looked at the time and decided she better get some food for Frank, so she dressed and headed for the hospital. First she needed to pick up a few things at the grocery store.

Marcia arrived at the hospital feeling like a giddy schoolgirl. She grabbed the two bags of groceries and slipped down to the basement.

Frank was patiently waiting for her, wandering around through her old office, looking for something to read.

She brought in the groceries, dropped them on the counter, and immediately went to ravage him. Again, he did things to her in ways she had always wanted but could not articulate in words. It was as if he were inside her mind or could read her thoughts.

Although this encounter was fairly quick, it was filled with a passion Marcia experienced only with Frank. She treated Frank to a quick shower and then started to prepare some oatmeal for him. She was still floating from the encounter as she poured the instant oatmeal into a plastic bowl and warmed it in the microwave. As it warmed, Marcia sliced an apple and served it to Frank. He enjoyed the simple but filling meal.

The connection between Marcia and Frank was quickly becoming more that just raw sex fulfilling their animalistic desires; it was starting to affect both of them on an emotional level. Marcia knew she had to go to work, so she reluctantly bid farewell to Frank and told him she would be back later to check on him.

Frank made himself comfortable on the old couch in the small break room off to the side. He now had enough food to last him a couple of days, and he realized he shouldn't eat it all at one time. With the microwave and TV working, he was good to last the rest of the week without assistance.

But he knew she would be back as soon as she could, so he relaxed and watched television for a little while. After he had had enough reality television, he decided to finish looking around in her office.

As he glanced around, he found a small bookshelf tucked in the corner and covered by an old sheet. The shelves were filled with medical books, journals, and scientific research articles. In her closet, he found boxes and boxes of Marcia's research documented by years and then separated by months within each box. Each box was labeled with the month and year the research started and the month and year it ended. Below each of the dates, was either the word "failure" or the word "success." Frank shifted around the boxes until he found the oldest box with the word "success."

"This should be interesting reading," he thought. Frank spent the next four-plus hours so fascinated by Marcia's research that he simply couldn't put it down. The odd thing was, he somehow understood the medical terms, but he couldn't understand why. The more he read, the more connected he felt to Marcia. He kept reading until Marcia interrupted him several hours later.

"Why are you into my research material?" Marcia inquired as she interrupted him. Frank looked up at her with almost a robotically curious look on his face. Beside him were a couple of open medical books on cryogenics. Marcia recognized the books that she used for her continuing-education program.

"You can't be serious!" she said, half laughing. Frank continued to look at her but now started to crack a smile.

"It took me years of medical school and doctoral-level work to understand what's in those books. Do you understand the concepts that are in these books?" she asked as she picked up a couple of them.

Again, Frank looked at Marcia and smiled. Then he nodded his head slowly.

"What about my research? Do you understand what I've been doing?"

Another slow nod indicated he understood.

"Well, feel free to read all you want. My material is already archived on the hospital's server. I just can't bring myself to throw this stuff away, so I hoard it all here, out of the way."

Frank went back to his reading.

"I've got to run some more tests, but I don't have the time right now. Frank, I'm going to draw some blood samples and get them analyzed, OK? Meet me over at the table." Marcia left her office and went to one of the many cabinets to retrieve a couple of test tubes and a syringe.

As she was sorting out the equipment, Frank approached her from behind and cuddled her. She went from all business to melting in his arms.

After a few long seconds, Marcia opened her eyes and forced herself to get serious about having to draw his blood.

Marcia sat him down and wrapped his biceps with a twelve-inch piece of rubber hose to ensure she would get a good flow of blood. As she tied off the rubber hose, she couldn't help but admire his toned muscles. After drawing the vials of blood, she applied a bandage and told him he was all set. Marcia labeled and stored the vial in a small fridge and prepared to leave.

You could tell he didn't want her to go. He gave her one of those puppy-dog looks that melted her heart.

"I've got to get him out of here and into a suitable place to stay," she thought as they embraced. Marcia slipped out the door and went down the hallway to work.

Chapter 19
MOVING DAY

Marcia was at work, but her mind was on what to do with Frank. She continued to wrack her brain throughout the day, thinking about the rehab center and the hotel option.

She knew she had to have a solution by the end of the day, because Zack was coming home and was going to take her on a romantic weekend at—suddenly, it dawned on her. "What about our cottage near Solomon's Island?" she finally said out loud. She caught herself speaking aloud and stopped, but it was too late.

"Dr. Gage, did you say something?" inquired one of her assistants.

"No, no. Sorry. I was just thinking out loud. Thanks for asking," Marcia responded.

"Oh, OK." The assistant paused at Marcia's office door for a few seconds.

"Is there something else?" Marcia asked.

"I was just wondering if you'd heard from Angie, Dr. Gage."

Marcia paused for a few seconds while she contemplated how to respond. She knew Angie was dead, and her body was stuffed in a steel vat just down the hallway right next to her boyfriend, but she had to remain calm and casual with her answer.

"No. That is kind of strange, isn't it? I can't remember a time in these last couple of years that we've worked together that she just up and disappeared without telling us that she was going somewhere," Marcia responded.

"Yes, that is strange," her assistant replied.

There was an awkward pause. Then Marcia broke the silence. "I need to get going."

"OK, Dr. Gage," the assistant replied and went back to work.

Marcia realized she had only four hours to get Frank to their cottage at Solomon's Island and back to the house with dinner before Zach arrived home.

In moments, she and Frank were on their way, but she had to stop by her home to pick up the key to the cottage and get some linen and supplies.

She parked her car in the garage and told Frank to stay put. He nodded, showing he understood. Marcia rounded up some sheets and blankets quickly but was having a hard time finding the key to the cottage. As she searched the downstairs office, she thought she heard footsteps going upstairs. She ran to the garage to find that Frank was not in the car.

She ran upstairs to find Frank standing at the foot of her bed and staring at the wedding picture of her and Zach on the nightstand. As she approached him from behind, he extended his right arm and opened his hand to expose the key she was looking for.

She didn't even bother to ask how he knew where the key was located. By now, she took it for granted that somehow he knew everything about her and knew everything she knew.

She gently took the key, and he motioned her toward the bed. Marcia shook her head and said, "No, not here...never here."

She knew over the last week, she had slipped to a new low in morality between what she allowed to happen to Angie and Tim and the fact that she had had sex with Frank.

But she was not going to have sex with Frank in the bed she shared with Zach. She was losing herself, but she still wanted to hold on to just a little bit of morality.

She took Frank's hand and led him downstairs. Once there, she handed him a paper bag filled with food she had taken from the pantry and said, "We need to go."

Forty-five minutes later, Marcia and Frank were pulling up to a quaint cottage nestled a quarter mile off a back road into the woods. Her grandmother had willed her the cottage, but since she wasn't much for rodents and insects, she and Zach had not spent much time out there. In fact, since their schedules got so out of control at work, it had been over a year since she had visited the property. It was in good shape thanks to a maintenance person they paid to check on the property and clean it once every three months. As she entered the cottage, she saw the caretaker had recently been there cleaning the place. There was not a speck of dust, and it smelled nice and clean. Marcia couldn't believe she had forgotten about using this place. It was perfect for Frank.

Realizing she had to hurry if she wanted to get home before Zach, she hastily showed Frank around, gave him a prepaid mobile phone she had picked up at the gas station on the way there, and told him he needed to stay there. "You have enough food for a couple of days. I will check on you tomorrow. This is my number already programmed into the phone. Call me if you need anything."

Frank nodded, indicating he understood. He gave her a warm hug that caused her to almost melt in his arms. Marcia slowly and reluctantly peeled herself from his grip, gave him a kiss on his cheek, and left. Tears rolled down her cheeks as she drove home.

Chapter 20
HELL TO PAY

Marcia arrived home with just enough time to clean up the house and shower. She'd hoped to have time to cook the meal she'd promised him. But realizing she didn't have enough time, she picked up some curried shrimp and shrimp fried rice on the way home. Not exactly a gourmet meal, but she knew Zach would enjoy it.

Zach arrived home to a warm welcome from Marcia. He wasn't sure what to expect given the last conversation on the phone, so he was pleasantly surprised when Marcia greeted him with a huge hug and a long kiss.

"I guess you *did* miss me after all," Zach said with a big smile as he handed her some flowers.

"Of course I missed you. I just had a stressful week without you. You know I don't sleep well when you're not home. These flowers are lovely," Marcia responded.

Zach heard her comment on the flowers, but was focused on why she seemed so distant over the phone. "Was that all it was?"

"Of course, of course," Marcia responded, trying to be reassuring. "I already have a bath drawn for you. Why don't you go in and relax?"

With that welcome, Zach grabbed his bags and made his way into the house with Marcia close behind.

"I'll warm up your dinner," Marcia yelled at him as he climbed the stairs.

"Awesome. Thanks. I'll just soak for a few minutes."

Fifteen minutes later, they were having dinner and sharing a bottle of wine. Marcia was feeling a little guilty about having been with Frank, and, to take the edge off, she was literally gulping down her glasses of wine. The wine was helping to douse the guilt and was making her feel a little sexy and flirty. Zach was picking up on the vibes, and, having spent all week in a hotel room by himself, he was ready for some loving from Marcia.

After dinner and two bottles of wine, they worked their way up to the bedroom and made passionate love. In the heat of lovemaking, Marcia had visions several times of being in the cottage where she'd dropped Frank off earlier. When they finished, they snuggled with their backs to each other and went to sleep. It didn't take long since they were both pretty much drunk.

Across town, at the cottage, Frank was awakened in the same moment that Marcia had her orgasm. He sat there in bed, sweating and knowing that Marcia was having sex with Zach. Frank felt connected to Marcia, and he was not about to have Zach keep her from him. He got up, got dressed, and made his way toward the old barn. In there was an old truck that had belonged to Marcia's grandfather that was also maintained by their maintenance person. It wasn't part of the contract they had with him; but every so often, he would ask Marcia to sell it to him in the hopes that one day, she would break down and part with it. Marcia had many fond memories of riding in the old truck with her grandfather, so she had a hard time parting with it. The caretaker knew he would eventually wear Marcia down enough to sell him the truck. Over the past year, she went from no way was she going to sell the truck to telling him if she decided to sell it, he would have the first right of refusal. In the meantime, he didn't want it to deteriorate, so he kept it in good running order pro bono.

The keys were under the truck's visor, and when Frank attempted to start the truck, nothing happened. He raised the hood and realized the battery was disconnected. After connecting the battery, the truck started on the first attempt. Frank was at the Gages' home and back in less than two hours.

Frank reset the alarm code, removed his blood-soaked clothes, tossed them into the back of the truck, and drove back to the cottage naked, unphased by the thirty-degree November weather. On his way, he saw a barrel fire in front of a service station and stopped long enough to throw his clothes and the large knife he used to kill Zach, into the fire before continuing on his way. After parking the truck and returning to the cottage, he scrubbed himself obsessively clean and got dressed in a set of Marcia's grandfather's clothes that he had found in a chest. He went back to bed and slept like a baby.

Marcia woke up in the morning, still a little tipsy, but quickly sobered when she realized she was soaked in Zach's blood. She touched him and felt a cold stiff shoulder. She knew he was dead. Her blood-curdling scream was loud enough to be heard by the neighbors.

Marcia was about to pay for Frank's killing spree.

Chapter 21
GUILTY AS CHARGED

Marcia called the police, but they had already received calls from two of her neighbors, who were now knocking at her door. Marcia opened the door in a gown drenched in blood that was starting to dry. She was shaking uncontrollably.

"What happened? What happened?" the neighbors both yelled. "Are you OK? Where's Zach? Did he do this?"

For a moment, Marcia just shook her head from left to right to everything they asked. Finally, she blurted out, "He's dead. Zach's dead. Oh my God, he's dead."

Just as they got her out of the house, two patrol cars arrived on the scene.

Seeing Marcia covered in blood, the senior sergeant went directly toward her and asked, "Are you hurt?"

Marcia shook her head from side to side.

"Who did this?"

No answer.

"Is someone hurt in the house?"

Before Marcia could answer, one of her neighbors said, "Her husband is dead inside the house."

"Who did it?" the officer immediately asked.

"We don't know. We just got here."

"Is anyone else in the house?" the officer asked Marcia.

Marcia was crying and simply swung her head from left to right.

The sergeant motioned to the other officer, who immediately got a blanket from the patrol car's trunk, covered Marcia, and then sat her in the patrol car.

While he was taking care of her, the sergeant called for backup and an ambulance.

In less than five minutes, two additional patrol vehicles and an ambulance arrived. By now, the first officer had gotten the names and contact information of the neighbors and instructed them to return to their homes. As the backup officers arrived, they fanned out in front of the home and cordoned off a one-hundred-foot area in front of the house. The vehicle with Marcia was moved to the end of the street, and the junior officer started asking her more questions to determine what was going on in the home. At the same time, the medical professionals were checking her over to determine if she had any wounds.

That information was passed to the other officers. But although they seemed to be no immediate danger in the Gages' home, they entered cautiously and were prepared in the event they encountered any violence.

They worked their way upstairs to the master bedroom after doing a sweep of the first level of the house and the other two upstairs bedrooms.

As they entered the master bedroom, they saw Zach's body and the blood-soaked sheets. The sergeant checked for a pulse and found none.

They had seen enough to determine this was a crime scene. After a quick sweep of the bathroom and closets to ensure the house was secure, they departed the home and waited for the crime investigation team and the coroner.

The police took Marcia to the hospital where she worked. Upon arriving at the hospital, she met an investigator who informed her he needed to take her gown and take some blood samples for evidence and asked if she objected. She agreed to be cooperative and gave them everything they needed. After all, her husband had been murdered, and she was completely innocent.

At her request, a security officer accompanied one of the emergency room nurses to Marcia's office to retrieve a set of scrubs, so she had something to wear.

Upon learning she worked at the hospital, the investigator asked if she knew Angie Warner, who also worked at the hospital.

"Yes, she was—I mean, is—my assistant," Marcia replied.

"Really," stated the investigator. "Have you seen her in the last couple of days?"

"No. She didn't show up a couple of days ago. I don't know why."

"How about Tim Sharpe? Do you know him?"

"Who is Tim Sharpe?" Marcia inquired.

"He's Angie's live-in boyfriend. We are having trouble finding him too. Have you seen him?"

"No. Why would I?"

Detective Thomas could hear the crack in her voice when she responded. He'd been on the force for over twelve years, and he didn't believe in coincidences. The fact that Marcia Gage was in the middle of a situation with two missing people and a dead husband was too much for him to ignore. The fact that she started to say Angie *was* her assistant wasn't lost on him either. His instincts told him Marcia knew more than she was telling him.

"You know what, Dr. Gage? Would you mind coming down to the station and making a statement? It's just procedure. I just need a statement while everything is still fresh in your mind." He could see her hesitation. "Look, I'll give you a ride to the station, escort you back to your home to pick up a few necessities, and I'll take you to a family member or friend. You can't go back in your house by yourself for the next few days anyway. My guys are processing your home as a crime scene."

Marcia decided to cooperate. She really didn't want to go but figured if she refused or asked for a lawyer, she would arouse suspicion. Little did she know, Detective Thomas considered her a person of interest and was already planning to get a warrant to investigate the use of her access card in and out of the hospital and to trace her cell phone and the cell phones of Angie and Tim.

While Marcia changed, Detective Thomas instructed his assistant to contact a judge to get a warrant to request access to Marcia's hospital key card records and her cell phone records. To determine if Marcia and Angie were in the same place at the same time, he also asked for Angie's hospital key card records and her cell phone records.

While he had Marcia at the station, the warrants came through, and the hospital quickly cooperated and provided the access records. The telephone records would take a few days.

As suspected, Detective Thomas found out both Angie and Marcia were in the hospital on the same day Angie was reported missing. In fact, the security officers told Detective Thomas they had both been in an unused section of the hospital during the week.

It was enough for Detective Thomas to ask Marcia, "Is there something you wish to tell me about what happened to Angie?"

Realizing the reason for her coming to the station had changed, Marcia became nervous and quickly said she wished to speak to a lawyer—at which time, Detective Thomas read Marcia her Miranda rights and told her she was being detained and that a lawyer would be provided.

Marcia was promptly processed and arrested, but no charges were filed yet. Detective Thomas knew he could hold her for only twenty-four hours without charging her, so he had to work fast.

He personally contacted the judge and requested a warrant to enter and search the "closed" section of the hospital that both Angie and Marcia had swiped into during the week.

At first the judge was reluctant, but he trusted Detective Thomas's instincts and granted the warrant.

Within hours, Thomas and his partner were back at the hospital and, with a security guard, entered the old office spaces.

As they entered, Thomas looked at the security officer and said, "I thought this area wasn't being used anymore."

"I didn't either," responded the guard.

It was obvious that the area had been recently used. Additionally, Marcia's key card showed multiple daily accesses. The security database also showed Angie had been in the area several times.

Their search of the area led them to a large freezer. They opened it and immediately noticed two metal vats near the entrance.

"We need to open these. Can you get someone who knows what to do to give us access?" Detective Thomas asked.

The security guard radioed dispatch, and, within a few minutes, someone was knocking at the door. The guard let her in. It was the assistant who had spoken with Marcia the previous day.

The assistant followed a four-step procedure and opened the first vat. As she opened it, she gasped with horror. Detective Thomas thought that was an unusual reaction from a person who worked with dead bodies on a regular basis.

"It's Angie, isn't it?" he asked before looking into the vat.

She nodded her head. "Yes," she cried.

Detective Thomas glanced in and saw that Angie was still wearing her lab coat.

After giving the assistant the opportunity to gather herself for a few minutes, the detective asked her to repeat the process for the second vat.

She opened it and looked in to see a naked man. As he looked at him, she realized he was Angie's boyfriend from the pictures she'd shown her on her phone.

"Do you know who he is?" the detective asked.

"It's Angie's boyfriend, Tim."

"Thanks. Look, we've put you through enough. Thanks for helping us. I need you not to mention anything you witnessed here today."

The assistant nodded and departed, still trying to pull herself together.

"This is now a crime scene," Detective Thomas said out loud.

His assistant knew what to do and went to work making several phone calls.

Detective Thomas made a call to the district attorney informing him of their findings. From there, the process to formally charge Marcia for the murders of Zach, Angie and Tim was in motion.

Detective Thomas arrived at the police station in time to tell both Marcia and her attorney what they planned to charge her with and the fact that they were going to transport her to the county jail.

Marcia was in handcuffs and was escorted outside to the police car. As she walked across the parking lot to the police vehicle, she was thinking, she had to get to Frank. She was worried about him surviving without her. When she saw her chance, she made a run for it. Being a runner, she had the speed to get away from the slightly heavy officer, so she was out of the parking lot in a flash. She bolted across the three-lane road, and was able to narrowly dodge two vehicles, only to be hit by the car in the third lane. Her body catapulted some twenty feet as the car's brakes screeched to a stop.

As Marcia lay in the middle of the street, her pulse raced. She knew she was seriously hurt and dying. In that moment, she knew she was communicating with Frank as her view changed from the icy street to the inside of the cabin. She knew he could hear her. As her life slipped away, the officer on the scene tried to make her comfortable by holding Marcia's hand and telling her to "hang in there; help is on the way." He kept talking to her to keep her awake and focused on him. The officer saw Marcia's lips moving, so he stopped talking long enough to hear her whisper.

"Come get me, Frank. Come get me. I want to live...aargh." Her last breath left her before she finished her final word, "Again."

Marcia died in the middle of the icy cold street.

Chapter 22
GRAVE ROBBERY

The first Friday after her death, a funeral was held for Marcia. Given the conditions under which she died, her family wanted a quick funeral that minimized the embarrassment of her being accused of killing her assistant, her assistant's boyfriend, and her husband. The police had informed them there were no traces of forced entry, and the alarm system had been turned off briefly on the night in question, indicating either Marcia allowed someone into the home to kill her husband or disarmed it as a means to blame someone else. Either way, the conditions under which she died were an embarrassment to her family, so a quick, quiet funeral was the way to go. The family elected not to have a viewing, so Marcia's body was transported from the coroner's freezer to the casket. There was a short service in the church followed by what seemed like another service by the grave site. Father Odom spent another fifteen minutes providing a eulogy at Marcia's grave while the few family and friends who attended suffered through an unexpectedly bitter cold snap in the middle of November.

The gravediggers, Pete and Richard, swiftly prepared to bury Marcia after her family and friends left the area. After Pete went to store the plants and miscellaneous materials from the grave site, Richard worked on releasing the lock that kept the casket in place over the grave. Thanks to Father Odom's long sermon, the lock for the automatic casket lowering system had frozen in place. Richard was so engrossed with fidgeting with the locking system that he didn't pay attention to Frank approaching him from behind. When the footsteps stopped, he turned to see who it was—just in time for his forehead to make contact with Frank's shovel.

The contact was so sudden and violent that it drove him backward, causing the back of his head to hit the frozen grass. He was barely conscious and lay bleeding and motionless on the ground. He wanted to move but didn't have the wherewithal to do anything but lie there, slowly drifting into unconsciousness. He felt searing pain throughout his head and down his back.

Blood trickled past his eyes as he watched in horror as Frank removed Marcia's frozen body from the casket.

When Pete returned a few minutes later, he found his coworker lying on the ground, barely alive, and the casket tipped over on its side. As Pete provided assistance, he used his cell phone to call for an ambulance. He initially assumed that the automatic lowering system failed, causing the casket to topple and hit Richard in the head.

But as he spoke to the 911 agent, his eyes widened in shock as he noticed the casket was empty. Only a broken half-inch sprig of a dark-purple Limonium plant remained in place of the corpse. As he looked around for answers as to what had happened, in the distance, Pete saw Frank carrying the body into the woods next to the cemetery.

When Frank made it to Marcia's grandfather's truck, he laid her body gently in the bed. Lining the truck's bed were pillows that he had removed from the couch at the cottage. He knew keeping her body frozen was best for her right now. After he laid her in the truck, he covered her with a blanket to ensure no one would see her as he drove down the street.

On his way to the cemetery, Frank had stopped a couple of blocks from Marcia's house and entered through her back door, using a key the Gages hid under an outdoor stereo speaker. He was able to slip inside and retrieve Marcia's hospital badge from her vehicle. He had counted on the fact that no one had set the alarm and that the police had not turned the home over to relatives yet, since they were still collecting evidence to close the case.

His hunch was right, and now he had Marcia's badge and her body and was headed to her lab at the hospital. As he drove, he realized he had a pretty good idea from all the research materials he'd read about how to bring her back, but he wasn't sure of the sequence of the procedures that had worked for him. He started concentrating on trying to recall a memory that wasn't his.

It was Marcia's memory.

As he focused, his eyes starting flickering rapidly to the point where he could not see, causing him to barely miss colliding head-on with another car. As he pulled over to the side of the road, his eyes continued to flicker. Then he shook as if he had been hit by a jolt of electricity. His crystal-blue eyes opened wide and stared into the distance.

It was obvious. He had found her memory...he knew what to do.

Frank continued down the highway as he looked at the clock. It was 6:00 p.m. on a Friday. He had sixty hours before Monday morning, when Marcia's team would start showing up at work. He set the timer on the watch he had taken from Angie's boyfriend, Tim, to count down the hours.

Frank knew he had to hurry.

Made in the USA
Middletown, DE
03 July 2021

43598772R00087